TRAPPED

Just as he finished saddling the last horse, Drew heard a sound like two boards slamming together. At the same instant, he heard Melissa scream.

His nerves tensed and he had the gut feeling that their time had just run out. With the other bedroll still in his hand, Drew whirled around, but he wasn't ready for what he saw.

Leaning nonchalantly against the front of the shack was Cap Dayton! His arms were crossed loosely over his thick chest and he wore a sneering smile. Drew looked around quickly for the other two brothers, but they were nowhere to be seen.

Then he remembered Melissa's scream. That meant that Tom and Slade were inside the shack with her!

Drew made a slight movement to draw his gun, but Cap drew his Colt .45 with such lightning speed that Drew froze where he stood. . . .

READ THESE ACTION-PACKED NOVELS OF THE FRONTIER WEST

MASSACRE AT WOUNDED KNEE (542, $2.50)
by Abby Mann
Spurred by the brutal killing of an old Indian, young radical leaders convince their fellow Indians to make a stand for their rights. They begin a peaceful hunger strike which ends in a violent, useless battle reminiscent of the age-old MASSACRE AT WOUNDED KNEE.

RIMROCK (576, $1.95)
by Don P. Jenison
When Lon rides into Bar S and discovers his father dead—shot in the back and left for the buzzards—he plots his revenge. If the law doesn't get the man who murdered his pa, his blazing sixguns will!

GUNN #1: DAWN OF REVENGE (594, $2.25)
by Jory Sherman
Accused of killing his wife, William Gunnison changes his name to Gunn and begins his fight for revenge. No sacrifice is too great. He'll kill, maim, turn the west blood red—until he finds the men who murdered his wife.

SHOWDOWN AT FIRE HILL (560, $1.95)
by Roe Richmond
After being forced to kill a bandit who'd once been his friend, Ranger Lashtrow wanted to lay down his guns. But deadly gunnies wouldn't let him run away, and he knew, sooner or later, he'd be back behind a gun barrel—even if it killed him.

Available wherever paperbacks are sold, or order direct from the Publisher. Send cover price plus 50¢ per copy for mailing and handling to Zebra Books, 21 East 40th Street, New York, N.Y. 10016. DO NOT SEND CASH!

THREE DAYS TO TUCSON
BY ERLE ADKINS

ZEBRA BOOKS

KENSINGTON PUBLISHING CORP.

ZEBRA BOOKS

are published by

KENSINGTON PUBLISHING CORP.
21 East 40th Street
New York, N.Y. 10016

Copyright © 1980 by Erle Adkins

All rights reserved. No part of this book may be reproduced in any form or by any means without the prior written consent of the Publisher, excepting brief quotes used in reviews.

Printed in the United States of America

Chapter One

The scorching rays of the late afternoon July sun beat relentlessly down on Fort Rather, Arizona, as Drew Williams walked across the parade ground in a loose-jointed gait, leading his horse. He'd been in the saddle all day and was bone tired. His broad shoulders drooped in fatigue.

"Hey, Drew," a voice called out and he glanced toward the corral where two soldiers were brushing their horses, "the old man wants to see you on the double."

"One of these days, Pete," Drew said with a weary grin as he slowly walked toward them, "Colonel Walters is going to hear you call him that and he'll skin you alive. What does he want this time?"

"Now you know he ain't in the habit of takin' privates into his confidences," the young soldier drawled. "All he said was tell you he wanted to see you in his office as soon as you got here."

Pushing his cap back on his head, the young private hooked his thumbs under his black suspenders. "Man, I wouldn't have your scoutin' job fur nuthin'. I like to be led where I'm goin'. Let somebody else worry about gettin' there."

"Heck, I would," the other soldier said, glancing around at Pete and resting his arms on top of the corral, the brush dangling in his hand. "You just ain't got no ambition, Pete. I wouldn't mind bein' an army scout if the pay is enough." Turning back to Drew, he squinted his eyes in the glaring sun and asked: "Just how much does it pay, Drew?"

"Well, Tommy," Drew answered, cocking an eyebrow at the youngster and remembering his own idea about money when he was about seventeen, "it pays just enough to make you risk your neck tracking Indians and leading wagon trains." He pushed his sun-streaked brown hair back from his weathered brown face and clamped a well-worn black flat-crowned hat back on.

"Better go see what kind of bee Walters has in his bonnet this time," Drew muttered irritably to himself as he walked with long strides back across the parade ground, kicking up dust with his moccasin boots. As he went across the yard, the rays on his back felt like the sun was beating out a vengeance on him. There was hardly a breath of air stirring. The flag drooped limply, like an old rag, on the iron pole in the middle of the yard and a film of dust covered the cannons on each side of it.

Williams stomped up on the porch in front of the colonel's office, dust flying from his feet.

"The colonel wants to see me," Drew told

the young corporal as he stepped inside, closing the door in a slam behind him.

"Yes, sir, I know," the young man replied mildly, a bemused expression in his eyes. "He's been lookin' for you for the past hour."

"That man would want me to hurry back from my own funeral," Drew said, shaking his head.

"If that's Williams out there," boomed a voice behind the door that was marked 'Colonel' on a burned piece of wood, "tell him to get his carcass in here."

"Still his usual sweet self, I hear," Drew said, grinning down at the lad.

"Yes, sir," the corporal replied, smiling back at him and shaking his head, "he is." Lowering his voice so that only Drew could hear, he asked, "Reckon he was born that way?"

"I wouldn't be a bit surprised," Drew said, slapping him on the shoulder, "no man could get that ornery in just a few years."

Drew opened the door, closed it behind him, and dropped his lanky frame on a chair facing the colonel.

Drew always felt smothered when he came into this office. It was a small room and every inch of space was used. A map of the Arizona Territory covered the entire wall behind the colonel's desk.

Two unsheathed sabers, with gold tassels on the handles, hung crossed under a confederate hat and a rebel flag. A lamp, suspended on chains from the bare raftered ceiling, hung over a littered desk. A bookcase was stacked with papers every which way and a safe took up the other side of the room. A double-doored closet was at the other end of the room.

"You took your own fine time in getting here," Colonel Walters complained in a high-pitched southern voice, his little blue eyes snapping. Leaning back in a swivel chair that was in bad need of oiling, he tapped his short and stubby fingers together.

"I got here as soon as I knew that you wanted to see me," Drew said wearily. He knew that Walters had another job for him to do. Walters wasn't the kind of person to just sit and talk about anything, unless it was New Orleans.

Drew didn't mind the work. He liked being outdoors and enjoyed the responsibility of his job. But the colonel always took his own good time in telling him what he wanted. It was at times like this when Drew had trouble deciding whether or not he liked Walters.

Drew didn't like George Walters when he was in one of his demanding and belligerent moods, as he was now. He liked him when he was happy and jovial. But the demanding moods usually overshadowed the others.

Drew blamed these moods on the colonel's age. He was getting on in years and resented the youth around him. The last time anybody knew his age, he was about sixty and that was at least five years ago.

Drew didn't know it but the colonel was a little jealous and envious of him. He envied Drew's youthful years of twenty-two. He envied Drew's wiry build, the broad shoulders that tapered down to a lean waist and narrow hips.

The colonel was short and a little on the pudgy side from lack of enough exercise. He was almost bald and what little hair he did have around the edges was gray. Also he had to use glasses to see. Each time that Drew returned from a scouting trip, the colonel always silently pretended that it was he doing something adventurous and dangerous, as he had Drew give explicit details of every job he went on.

"Is this going to take long?" Drew asked impatiently, standing up.

"It might," the colonel snapped and glared at him. "Sit down." Drew unhooked the heavy gun belt, dropped it on the floor, and sank down again in the armless chair.

"Now tell me what you want me to do," he said. "I know this can't be a social visit."

"I think this is going to be one of the most pleasant jobs I've ever had you do," the coloonel said. A twinkle replaced the glare in his blue eyes.

"Pleasant?" Drew repeated skeptically, holding his breath. "Don't tell me I'm going to take you back to New Orleans," he said hopefully.

The colonel was always talking about the day when he could retire and return to New Orleans. He hadn't been home in a few years. But the way he always reminisced to anyone who'd listen about the glorious and gracious way of living before the war, anyone would think that there had never been a war and that he'd only just come from the crescent city.

It was at times like this when Drew didn't like the colonel, when he played guessing games.

"How do you mean 'pleasant'?" Drew asked again, watching the colonel intently.

"No, I'm not going back to New Orleans," Walters said wistfully. "Not just yet anyway. But someday. I'm sure that you've heard of Rance Dunbar?" he asked.

"Sure," Drew said, crossing his long legs. "He's the territorial senator. But what's so pleasant about him?"

"He's not the pleasant part," Walters said, laughing boisterously at Drew. "It's his daughter."

"I didn't know he had a daughter," Drew said with a shrug, not that it mattered one way or the other. He knew Walters would get around to telling him about her in his own way. But the picture of a little girl spoiled rotten with pigtails, freckles and buckteeth, popped into his mind.

"Well, his daughter has come out here from Philadelphia with a friend to see him," Walters said, "and I want you to take them from here to Tucson."

That's all I need, Drew thought, to play nursemaid to two little spoiled girls.

"Are you kidding?" Drew asked slowly, leaning forward in the chair and watching the colonel through narrowed eyes.

"No, I'm not kidding," Walters replied

sarcastically, "and here's why." He went on quickly knowing that Drew was going to argue with him. "I guess you know that Cap Dayton and his commanchero brothers have been giving guns to Chief Half Moon and his braves. The Indians, in turn, raid settlements and wagon trains, then divide the take with the Daytons for extra food and blankets."

The situation was becoming more confused. First, the senator's daughter. Then, outlaws and Indians. It wouldn't surprise Drew if a bunch of gypsies didn't end up in this.

"How were the Indians getting along for food before the Daytons conned them?" Drew asked, slumping down in the chair and pushing his hat back on his head.

"That's another thing," Walters said. "You know as well as I do that Indians have always depended on buffalo for everything they do. Since the Daytons have been supplying food for them, they naturally feel like they're entitled to the buffalo. So they kill them, skin them, and sell the hides. The meat goes to waste."

"Aren't there three Dayton brothers?" Drew asked, uncrossing his long legs and sitting up straight in the chair. He was becoming more interested. The colonel felt a little better about the situation now. At least Drew was asking questions.

"Yeah," Walters nodded, "Cap, Slade, and Tom. Do you know them?"

"Only by reputation," Drew answered. "I saw a poster on them somewhere. I understand they're really tough characters. But what does all of this have to do with me and Rance Dunbar's daughter?"

"Rance Dunbar," Walters explained patiently, "with the president's approval, has promised to help feed the Indians if they'll stop taking guns from the Daytons and stop raiding the settlements and wagon trains. Dunbar also promised to give them outdated guns to use just for hunting."

"Now you are joking," Drew said with a smile that lifted the corners of his thin-lipped mouth. "Why should the Indians take some old guns from the government when they can have brand new ones from the Daytons? Who's going to watch over the Indians to make sure the guns are used just for hunting?"

"I keep telling you, I'm not joking," Walters roared crossly, banging his fist on the desk. "One good reason that the Indians should take the old guns from the government is that there are no strings attached like there are with the Daytons. Half Moon is willing to sign an agreement with the government and all of his braves agree. They're tired of seeing the meat being wasted."

"Who's going to enforce such an agreement?" Drew asked dubiously, turning his head slightly and looking at Walters from the corner of his eye. "Who's going to tell the Daytons that their little party is over? Does Half Moon believe it'll work?"

"I guess he does," Walters answered. "He's coming here to meet Dunbar next week for the signing. As to your other question, the army will probably enforce it and the senator will have to tell the Daytons."

"Now that will make all the difference in the world," Drew said mildly, nodding his head. "I can just hear the Daytons saying, 'Yes, sir, Mr. Senator, sir. We'll do exactly what you say, sir. Go ahead and sign your little agreement with Half Moon and we'll tuck our tails between our legs, go off, and be good.' Colonel, these men aren't little boys to have their hands paddled when they're bad."

"The agreement will work," Walters persisted, slamming his fist against the desk again and ignoring the sarcasm in Drew's voice.

"Well," Drew continued, drawing his black eyebrows together in a frown, "what does Dunbar's daughter and her friend have to do with the buffalo and the Daytons and going to see her father?"

"I'm getting to that," Walters said peevishly, pushing aside an array of papers and resting his elbows on the desk. "The word is out that the Daytons have sworn to kidnap Senator Dunbar's daughter to keep him from signing the agreement with Half Moon." Walters looked Drew directly in the eye and pronounced each word carefully.

"If Dunbar is going to meet Half Moon here next week, why can't his daughter wait here where she'll be safe?" Drew asked, still frowning. "Why didn't she go to Tucson from Philadelphia?"

"She thought the senator was going to be here to meet her and they were going back to Tucson together," Walters said. "But something happened and he couldn't leave Tucson. As to why she can't wait here, her father is having a birthday in three days and she's already made plans for his party in Tucson."

"It'll take at least three days to get from here to Tucson," Drew pointed out, standing up. "It took longer to come here from Philadelphia. How did she get this far without me and who's this friend of hers?"

The idea of a little girl left his mind. A little girl wouldn't give such details for a party. Maybe a teenager. That's just as bad, though, he thought. Teenagers are more hard-headed than children.

"You can ask more questions than an old maid school teacher," the colonel said crossly. "They came here by train as far as Santa Fe and the rest of the way by stage under an armed guard." When surprise at the mention of an armed guard widened Drew's eyes, Walters continued, "There was a gold shipment on the stage, and when they found out who she was, they let them come with them. The friend is a young man Dunbar met in England two years ago. He invited him to come over here and see some of this country, and before you ask, I don't know why Dunbar was in England."

"Why can't you send them to Tucson with an escort?" Drew asked.

"For one thing, I can't spare the men," Walters said. "But I've got to use the best means available getting them there and you're it. With your scouting experience, you could spot any trouble before it happened. Three people wouldn't cause much of a commotion. But an armed guard would."

Drew knew, to the colonel, the whole scheme sounded so simple. But when Indians and their way of life were involved with white men, nothing was simple. Except getting killed. That didn't take much trouble. Just be in the right or wrong place at the right or wrong time.

"Look, Colonel," Drew said pleadingly, leaning over and placing his hands palms down on the edge of the desk and bending forward, "you don't want to see a grown man cry, do you? I'll track Indians for you in the snow. I'll ride day and night after outlaws. But I don't know a thing about handling girls and I've never seen anybody from England. Couldn't . . . ?"

"No," Walters interrupted with a snap. "If you don't go willingly, I'll order you to and I can do it. Besides, you're the best man for the job." A cunning smile tugged at his full-lipped mouth.

Drew knew that the colonel was buttering him up. But he was as human as the next person and liked being flattered and told that he did a good job. He knew he'd give in. But not all at once.

"Why don't you just have the marshal arrest the Daytons?" Drew suggested.

"For what?" Walters asked sharply, leaning back in the chair and clasping his hands behind his head. "It's no crime to kill the buffalo. It would be hard as a rock to prove that the Daytons are giving guns to the Indians.

They could just say the Indians stole them. They haven't kidnapped the Dunbar girl yet. And anyway, they've been hiding out and nobody seems to know where. We can't even find them!"

Drew knew that it would do no good to argue with the colonel when his mind was already made up.

"Okay," Drew relented, shrugging his shoulders. "I'll take them. But only on one condition. That it's done my way."

"I don't care how you do it," Walters said with a wave of his hand. "Just as long as you get it done."

"Well, I guess it's time to see who I'm taking to Tucson," Drew said, sighing deeply. "By the way. How old is this little girl?"

"Oh," Walters said, looking up at the ceiling and bringing his gaze slowly back to Drew with a gleam in his eyes, "I'd say about eighteen or nineteen," spacing his words and smiling broadly at Drew. "Why?"

"Oh, I sort of had the idea that she was a little kid," Drew said truthfully. He felt a blush on his face as the colonel watched him. "A young lady. That's really all I need."

"My boy, you're in for a real treat," Walters replied, bursting out in laughter and slapping his hands together.

"Well, let's get it over," Drew said, sitting down in the chair again. "Send the corporal to get them."

Drew got up again and walked to the window. It wasn't long before he saw a girl and a young man coming from the guest quarters.

She walked with a quick, sure step, head held up high, and a straight back. With a gloved hand, she held her dress carefully up out of the dust.

Drew shook his head, switching his attention from the girl to the man walking beside her. He was dressed in tan Eastern riding clothes. The pants, with flared hips, had the legs stuffed down into boots that were laced halfway to the knees. He wore a hat that had undoubtedly caused a lot of comment after he crossed the Mississippi. It looked like a small brown saucer turned upside down with a high round top. He swung a short riding crop with such an arrogance that it brought a chuckle from Drew.

"I wonder if he could defend himself against Cap Dayton or Half Moon with that little switch?" Drew asked Walters who'd joined him at the window. "Is he what you meant by the surprise?" He turned to face the colonel who was smiling with a I'm-glad-it's-you-and-not-me grin.

"I wonder if he could defend himself against her with it?" the colonel added.

The corporal had beat the couple back to the office and stood up quickly as they came in.

"Will you be seated, please?" he requested formally. "I'll tell the colonel you're here."

"Well, really," the man said in the most English accent, in fact, the only English accent Drew had ever heard. "I thought you said that we were expected." He removed the small hat from black hair that was plastered to his head.

"It'll only be a minute, sir," the corporal said pleasantly, then escaped into the colonel's office.

Drew knew that secret observation was the best way to learn about people. All pretenses are dropped when people don't know that they're being watched. So stepping to the door, Drew opened it a tiny crack. He felt his heart squeeze as he saw the girl closer. His breath caught in his lungs. If someone had told him that he was suffering from the first pains of love, he'd have told them they'd been out in the blazing sun too long without a hat.

But he did know that she was the prettiest woman he'd even seen. Hair, the color of honey in sunlight, was caught back in curls from an oval face with high cheek bones and a firm jaw. A well-shaped mouth, which he didn't think smiled very often, curved under a turned-up nose. Her long-lashed brown eyes under black brows blended with a creamy skin. The only flaw on her face was a tiny black mole at the left side of her nose.

An emerald green velvet dress, trimmed in black satin, and a silly green hat with a feather in it added to her beauty.

"Charles, will you please sit down," she said in a soft voice to the young man pacing up and down the small waiting room.

"Well, really," he said irritably, stopping in front of her. "What can you expect? Being kept waiting by a colonel and an army scout," he continued indignantly as though the two terms were below his dignity.

"I know," she agreed peevishly as she began tapping her foot impatiently on the floor. Drumming her gloved fingers on the small black drawstring purse, she glanced quickly at the door she thought was closed, her brown eyes snapping. "Papa seems to know this colonel and holds him in high regard, and you know he said, when we got here today, that this scout knows what he's doing."

Drew turned around from the door and shot the colonel a hot look. A turkey for Christmas couldn't have looked any more stuffed than the colonel did when he heard the girl say that her father held him in high regard.

"Corporal," Drew said, clearing his throat and easing the door shut, "show them in."

"This way, ma'am," the corporal said, smiling and pushing the door open for them. She swept through the door without even a glance in his direction. The man passed him as though he wasn't there.

"Miss Dunbar," the colonel said, indicating the chair in which Drew had been sitting and turning to face him, "this is Drew Williams. He's going to take you and Mr. Sinclair to Tucson."

"Miss Dunbar," Drew said, smiling down at her. "Mr. Sinclair," he said, extending his hand. For a brief moment, Drew thought that Sinclair wasn't going to shake his hand. But for manners sake, Sinclair took Drew's hand in a somewhat limp grip.

As the colonel had introduced them, the girl turned her gaze fully on Drew. Her brown eyes ran over him as if she was sizing up a horse that she was going to buy. The glance started at his fringed moccasin boots, black pants, the legs inside the boots, and a blue shirt that had seen bluer and better days. When her eyes came to his face, her expression changed from boredom to surprise. Here she saw a handsome, lean jaw that needed a shave, a firm mouth that could probably smile as well as snarl. His thin nose that could have been broken at least twice and his blue eyes, holding an amused gleam, which was going to change her mind about army scouts. His hair wasn't really long, just below the collar of his shirt. But longer than she was used to seeing on the young men in Philadelphia and certainly longer than Charles Sinclair's.

"Colonel, I hope he's faster in getting us to Tucson than you were in seeing us," she purred in a soft, irritated voice, tearing her eyes from Drew and facing Walters, a cold expression in her eyes.

"He will be," Walters quickly assured her. There should be a reward for this, Walters told himself. With a daughter who looks like Miss Dunbar, the reward should be exceptional. "He will be," his high-pitched voice cracked.

"Well, Miss Dunbar," Drew said, trying to lighten the atmosphere, "what's your first name?"

"Not that it will matter," she said reproachfully, turning her gaze back to Drew, arching her eyebrows, and giving him a level look, "because I am and will be 'Miss Dunbar' to you, my first name is Melissa."

"Well, really," Sinclair gasped indignantly,

tapping the riding crop against his foot, "I presume that you will ask how old she is."

"No," Drew said, grinning broadly and holding his gaze, "I guess you judge people's age pretty much the same way you do a horse: by looking at their teeth. Miss Dunbar has nice-looking teeth and I'd guess that she's about nineteen years old."

"Well, really," Sinclair gasped horrified, his fair complexion turning pink. Melissa Dunbar's mouth flew open and her eyes widened. A red blush rushed from her neck all the way up to the silly green hat she wore. She'd never before been talked to or about in this uncivilized manner.

"Now before we waste any more time," Drew said slowly and cynically, sitting down on the edge of the desk, "I might as well tell you how we're going to be traveling. Miss Dunbar, I do hope you can ride a horse."

A cannonball or a fire arrow through the window couldn't have caused any more drastic reaction from Miss Dunbar and Sinclair than Drew's last statement.

"Well, really, Williams," Sinclair protested, "Miss Dunbar didn't come all the way out here on a stage to go horseback riding," still tapping the crop against his foot.

"Ride a horse?" she gasped, a hand at her throat. "I? The daughter of a senator? Ride a horse? No self-respecting lady that I know rides a horse. Not unless, of course, it's in a contest or a show."

She wasn't used to being asked questions and told what to do. She was usually the one in command and having people do her bidding.

Casting beguiling brown eyes up at Drew, she thought that statement took care of the whole matter. Usually one of her looks and statements as the one she'd just used on Drew took care of anything she didn't like.

"That's why it would be best to go on horseback," Drew said simply, a tight smile on his mouth. Melissa didn't believe it! She'd just said that a person in her position didn't go horseback riding unless it suited her.

"Do you ride, Sinclair?" Drew asked, turning his attention to the Englishman.

"Of course, I ride," Sinclair answered arrogantly, drawing himself up as tall as he could. Drew was six feet tall and Sinclair came just above his shoulders. Sinclair's light brown eyes held a contemptuous look as if it galled him to have to explain himself to a "frontiersman" such as the one sitting so nonchalantly before him. "I am a captain of one of the finest riding clubs in London."

"Well, then," Drew replied easily, clasping his hands together, "you should have no trouble handling a horse."

"But surely we could use a stage or a carriage," Melissa insisted in that same purring voice. "That would be so much better." She turned on a smile that had always worked on men before, young or old, at getting her way. But she'd never met a man like Drew Williams before.

"No, ma'am," Drew said, trying to ignore the smile. But it was awfully hard to do, especially when there were dimples at the corner of her mouth. "We go on horses."

"Well, then a pack animal will certainly have to be used to carry our things," Sinclair said emphatically, feeling very much the man of the moment. Maybe they could ride roughshod over a woman. But certainly not on a man who was used to giving orders as captain of one of London's best riding clubs. Melissa looked up at Drew, nodding her head in agreement, and batted her long lashes, seeing that the smile hadn't worked. She was certain that Charles would take care of things.

"Now listen," Drew said slowly, looking down at the floor and beginning to run out of patience. "If the Daytons are going to try anything, the faster we get you to your father, Miss Dunbar, the better. A pack horse is out of the question. It would only slow us down. The only clothes you should take with you is what you can put in a bedroll and saddle bag. Your other things can be sent on later. If you're coming back here next week, you won't need much anyway."

Once again the haughtiness came into Melissa's eyes as she raked her gaze over Drew, taking in his well-worn clothes, the sweaty hat, and the scuffed moccasins.

"Apparently," she said, a sneer curling her lips, "I change my clothes more often than some people do."

"I agree with Miss Dunbar, Williams," Sinclair interrupted quickly. "I always change my clothes at least twice a day. Especially before dinner each evening."

"That's fine," Drew replied flatly, looking

Sinclair directly in the eye, a frown drawing his eyebrows together. "If you can stick enough clothes in a saddle bag and bedroll for two changes in three day, be my guest."

It was just about all that Drew could do to keep from laughing at these two people. No doubt they'd always had life easy and had no idea what could be in store for them.

"Miss Dunbar," said the colonel, who'd been standing quietly all this time, "you might ride better if you wear a pair of..." He stopped, turning red, not knowing how to says pants or britches to a woman, especially one like Melissa Dunbar.

"The colonel's right, ma'am," Drew said quickly. If time had permitted, he would have let Walters stew a little and get out of his own predicament. But he added, "do you have a pair of trousers and a shirt?"

By this time, Melissa Dunbar was breathing hard, her chest rising and falling. Anger colored her face red. Her brown eyes bore into him like daggers. If she kept pulling on the draw strings of her purse so hard, Drew thought, they'll break. She'd never been talked to of such personal things before by men. As Drew's father would have said, she was mad enough to fight a brace of wild cats.

"Gentlemen," she said slowly and crisply, raising her head a little higher than it already was, "I always wear a dress."

"I do hope that you don't expect me to change the way that I am dressed," Sinclair said belligerently, a look of horror on his face.

"Only one suggestion," Drew said, looking

at the hat that Sinclair held so carefully in his long-fingered hands. "If you don't want your head and neck to burn to a crisp between here and Tucson, you'd better get another hat."

"I knew it," Sinclair stormed between clenched teeth and breathing harshly through flared nostrils. He gave his boot a sharp whack with the crop. "All I've heard since I've been in this barbaric country is derogatory remarks about my hat. I'll have you know that this is the type of hat that a properly dressed gentleman wears in England."

"Okay," Drew relented with a shrug. "Suit yourself. It's your neck." Drew knew that he wouldn't be caught anywhere outside without his big brimmed hat on to keep the sun off his neck.

"Drew," the colonel asked, wanting to hurry things along, "what time do you want to leave tomorrow?" He wanted to get his business over and be done with these two demanding people.

"We'll make more time if we leave before dawn," Drew answered. "About four, I guess." He stood up and strapped on his gun. Sinclair's brown eyes widened to almost twice the normal size and his face turned white when he saw the long-barreled, blue-plated pistol.

"Before dawn?" Melissa cried incredulously, looking Drew straight in the eye. "I refuse to go anywhere until the sun comes up and I'm able to see exactly where I'm going."

She smiled confidently, pleased with herself at telling a middle-aged colonel and a brash army scout what she would and wouldn't do. If she wasn't up at four, he'd just simply have to wait until she was up.

Melissa Dunbar had always gotten her way and she saw no reason why things should change now. She'd always had the best that money and her parents could afford. The best schools in Philadelphia were where she'd been educated. Plush hotels were hers when she traveled.

Now, here were two strangers, telling her that she'd have to get up before dawn and ride a horse to join her father. How ridiculous could anyone get? She'd show them!

But she'd never met anyone like Drew Williams before. She was to find out that he could be just as stubborn and willful as she was.

Sinclair still hadn't said anything about the early hour of departure. His eyes were still riveted on the gun strapped around Drew's waist. His breath came out in gasps and he gripped the crop in both hands.

As though the girl and the Englishman weren't in the small office, Drew turned to Walters. "Colonel," he said softly but sternly, "unless we do this my way and leave before dawn, you can get someone else to take Miss Melissa Dunbar, daughter of a senator, and this fancy friend of hers to Tucson."

"Miss Dunbar," the colonel cajoled, spreading his hands helplessly, knowing that Drew meant exactly what he said, "Drew's right. I telegraphed your father that the best man I had would take care of you. It will be best for all concerned if you do leave early. It won't be so hot and the horses can go further."

For a moment the girl sat silent. She didn't want to give in. It wasn't in her character to back down to anyone. But she saw a determination in Drew's blue eyes and decided that if she had to go on a horse, she would feel as safe with him as anybody. If he was this obstinate to her now, he would certainly stand up to someone lesser than she and wouldn't let anything happen to her and Sinclair.

"Oh, all right," she agreed, tossing her head, swallowing her pride and standing up. "Your mind is already made up anyway. If I'm going to have to get up at such an unreasonable hour, I must get some sleep."

Holding up her dress, she walked over to Sinclair, waiting for him to open the door. Her movement seemed to snap him out of the trance he was in. Shaking his head as though clearing his thoughts, Sinclair reached out for the door handle.

"Do you have to use that thing very often?" he asked, a weakness in his voice, looking slowly up at Drew after taking his gaze from the holstered Colt .45.

"No, not very often," Drew replied softly, feeling a little sorry for this man who was in a strange country that was governed by even stranger rules. Sinclair opened the door and he and Melissa left the office and crossed the fort's parade ground back to the guest quarters.

"Whew," the colonel whistled softly through his teeth, lowering himself heavily into his swivel chair. Taking a white handkerchief from his pocket, Walters wiped his face. "I'm glad that's over. I'd hate to be in your boots 'cause you're going to have your hands full." Pursing his full lips, Walters nodded his head slowly, his eyes gleaming.

"Oh, she's just spoiled and used to getting her own way," Drew said smiling, his blue eyes twinkling, "you've just got to show her who's boss. That's all. I've never been around women much. But I guess they're just like a stubborn mule. You've got to show them. As far as Sinclair, he's just plain scared to death. Did you see how he stared at my gun?"

The colonel nodded, threw back his head, and laughed. "I'm still glad that I don't have to be a guide for that spoiled girl and nutty Englishman."

"Well," Drew said, pulling his hat down and going to the door, "I'd better see about provisions." At the door, he turned back facing the colonel. "You wouldn't by any chance have an old hat that you don't need, would you? Sinclair's neck and head are going to burn right down to the bone with that stupid hat on."

"I think so," Walters answered. Getting up, he opened the closet door, reached way in the back, and pulled out an old wide-brimmed gray felt hat. "I haven't worn this hat in years," he said smiling fondly, handing the hat to Drew. There wasn't time for any of his reminiscences, so Drew quickly took the hat and closed the door behind him.

The corporal looked up as Drew came out of Walters' office. "I don't suppose you'd want to trade jobs, would you?" he asked, a sly grin spreading across his thin face.

"Oh, no," Drew replied, shaking his head. "That's some woman and with that Englishman along, this is going to be some trip."

Drew started toward the barracks where he slept when he was at the fort. But an idea struck him and he crossed to the opposite side of the fort to the tack room. A young boy was mending a saddle on the porch.

"Hey, Tag," Drew called out cheerfully, approaching the tall, thin youth, "want to earn a dollar?"

"Sure," the boy answered, stopping his work, hearing his name called. His green eyes lit up at the mention of money. "What do you want me to do? Put glue in the colonel's chair?"

"No, nothing like that," Drew said, laughing at the suggestion. "I want to buy a pair of your pants and a shirt." Reaching into his pocket Drew pulled out the necessary coin. "They don't have to be any of your best. Just some that you don't want. You might not get them back."

"For yourself?" Tag asked puzzled, looking Drew up and down. "You know you can't wear my clothes." In comparison, Drew would make two of the youngster who'd wandered into the fort about two years ago, telling them then that he thought he was fourteen. He'd never said where he was from or where he'd been going and seemed happy at the fort, always begging the men to let him go with them on patrol.

No matter what he ate, and the cook always saw that he had enough, his food just didn't stick to his ribs. Tag Hooper was as healthy as any boy his age should be. But his clothes always seemed to hang on him and were usually too short.

"No, they're not for me," Drew laughed, trying to picture Miss Melissa Dunbar in a pair of pants and a shirt, but somehow the image just wouldn't appear.

"Oh, by the way," Drew called out as Tag walked toward his room at the back of the tack shed, "would you happen to have an old hat you don't need?" Drew knew that Melissa, like Sinclair, would need a better protective hat at some point during the trip and Tag's hat would come near fitting her than his and he couldn't ask the colonel for another of his hats.

When Tag returned with the clothes and hat, his natural curiosity got the better of him.

"Drew, if I'm gonna sell you my clothes," he said, pushing his long blond hair back from his thin face, "I think I've got the right to know what you're gonna do with 'em"

In limited detail, because time was slipping by and there were several other things that had to be done, Drew explained about Miss Melissa Dunbar, Charles Sinclair, the senator, and the Dayton men.

"Golly, Ned!" the boy exclaimed, his eyes wide with excitement. "Ask Colonel Walters if I can go with you. I've heard about them Daytons. They're a mean bunch and I can help you. Ask him. Ask him."

"Now wait a minute, Tag," Drew said slowly.

He didn't want to hurt the boy's feelings. He could remember when he was Tag's age and the quest for adventure had surged through his veins. But he wouldn't have time to worry about Tag and take care of Melissa Dunbar and Charles Sinclair all at the same time.

"I know you'd be a big help, Tag," Drew said kindly. "But I'm afraid Miss Melissa Dunbar and Charles Sinclair would cramp your style. It'll be a handful just keeping her in line. I'll take you with me on my next trip. Okay?"

Drew couldn't have known it, but he would later regret what he'd just promised.

"Okay, Drew," Tag said, his voice low in disappointment. "It's just as well. I'm not too good around women anyway."

With the clothes and hats under his arm, Drew went to the mess hall. Joe, the cook, was used to Drew's comings and goings and fixing food sacks for him, so he didn't ask any questions. He just packed enough beans, dried meat, coffee, and flour to last four or five days.

One last thing remained to be done and that was to arrange for horses. He didn't know what kind of riders Melissa Dunbar and Sinclair were. Not many of the fort's horses were as gentle as he would have liked. But they would have to do with what was available.

"Hey, Pete," Drew called out to the private he'd been talking to earlier. "I need horses for a lady and an Englishman."

Pete came jogging toward him and called out, "Is she the one who came in around noon?" taking a rope from the fence.

"Yes," Drew answered. "I don't know if she can ride a horse very well, so cut out the gentlest one we've got."

"What kind of woman is she?" Pete asked, taking note of the silly smile on Drew's face.

"She's something, Pete," Drew answered, shaking his head a little. "A little on the spoiled side. But she's beautiful."

"Like that, huh?" Pete asked, Drew just nodded.

"The man claims that he was a member of a riding club in England," Drew said, "so he should be able to handle a horse pretty well. But just to be on the safe side, cut out a good one for him, too."

Drew really wasn't pleased with the two bays that Pete led back to him. But they would have to do. One was a little spirited and the other too big. Maybe Miss Dunbar could handle the spirited one better than the big one.

Drew thought about going back and talking more with Walters about the situation. But they would only rehash what had already been said.

Besides it was getting late. The sun was already creeping down behind the purple mountains. If they were to leave at four the next morning, he should be getting some rest.

So with apprehension and reservation on his mind, Drew kicked through the dust toward the barracks.

Chapter Two

Drew had always been an early riser and awoke at three the next morning. It was still pitch dark outside.

Melissa was the first thing on Drew's mind when his eyes opened. He could see her huge fiery brown eyes and the proud lift of her head and the dimple at the corner of her mouth as she smiled. He grinned, thinking how she'd tried to bully him and the colonel yesterday with that smile.

Remembering what she and Sinclair had said about cleanliness, Drew bathed and shaved as close as the razor would go without taking off an extra layer of skin. He put on fresh clothes and packed an extra change in the saddle bags.

Looking toward the guest quarters, he sucked in his breath in real surprise and was pleased to see light in two windows. Well, at least they're up, he thought. I hope they're dressed and packed. His heart beat faster just thinking of seeing Melissa soon.

Crossing the yard with his bedroll under his arm, he went first to the door that he'd seen her entering last night and knocked twice.

"Miss Dunbar," he called. Without waiting for her to answer, he continued, "It's four. Time to go."

"I'll be right there," he heard her reply sleepily as he walked down the porch to Sinclair's door.

"Sinclair," he said, rapping hard on the door. "It's time to go. Are you ready?"

"Yes. Of course," came the English-accented reply in a cold tone. "You told me to be ready at this unreasonable hour." Drew left the man talking, crossed to the corral, and saddled the three horses that had been left in a separate lot, tying a bedroll and water canteen to each saddle. He tied an extra canteen with his and stuck a Winchester rifle in a well-worn scabbard.

Not expecting Melissa to walk across the yard in the dark, Drew led the horses to where she and Sinclair stood. He wasn't surprised to see her wearing a dress instead of pants. She probably wouldn't give in to anything, Drew thought, shaking his head. Morning breezes brought a whiff of lilacs to him. He breathed deeply, filling his lungs with the delicate fragrance.

He couldn't tell exactly what color her outfit was. But he could see that it was of a light material. That will be one thing in her favor. The small hat, with a feather, perched on top of her head wouldn't be much protection from her face and neck in the blazing sun, though. But then he saw the frilly parasol. So she does listen to a little reasoning.

Sinclair was dressed the same as yesterday.

But undoubtedly in fresh clothes. He still wore the small hat and carried the riding crop. I wonder if he sleeps with it, Drew mused, grinning to himself.

"Would it be asking too much," Melissa asked sarcastically, "to put this dress in there?" pointing to the bedroll.

"No, ma'am," Drew replied, taking the tightly folded dress. He untied the blanket, laid the dress carefully inside, rerolled and retied the bedroll.

"If you will show me how to untie that contraption," Sinclair said contemptuously, "I'd like to put this outfit in it."

"Let me have it," Drew said, reaching for the clothes. "I'll show you how when it's light."

"This horse is the most gentle we have," Drew said, taking Melissa by the arm. "She's a little spirited but you can probably handle her better than the big one."

"I guess it will do," she said crisply as he bent down to take her small foot in his hand so that he could boost her up. He straightened, brushed the dust from his hands, and watched amazed as she crooked her right leg around the saddle horn. Something told him that it was going to be a long trip to Tucson.

Nearing the gate, she asked, "Aren't we going to have breakfast before we leave?"

"Ma'am, by the time we go to the mess hall," Drew answered patiently, "wake old Joe and have him fix breakfast, we could be several miles on the way."

"Well, really," Sinclair protested harshly,

riding close beside Melissa, "what are we supposed to do? Starve?"

"No. Nothing like that," Drew answered, suppressing a laugh. "We'll stop at sunup, rest the horses, and then eat."

"What time is sunup?" Melissa asked.

"Well, this is July," Drew answered, "and it's light earlier in the summer. So it shouldn't be too long."

Without saying anymore, she just grasped the reins and tightened her leg around the saddle horn.

They traveled the first few miles in complete silence. Drew never had been any good at small talk. To him, if words didn't accomplish something, they were useless. Besides, he didn't know anything to talk about.

He'd never been to Philadelphia and he certainly didn't want to go to England. With Sinclair along, Drew didn't think she'd want to talk to him anyway. So the only sounds, other than the crickets, cicadas, and wind, were the horses.

The rhythmical sounds of the creaking saddles and the horses' hooves on the dry, hard packed ground had a hypnotic effect on Drew and drowsiness settled over him and his eyelids grew heavy. He was used to sleeping in the saddle and dozed a couple of times. But the others stayed awake.

Drew had noticed that Melissa kept her horse close to Sinclair, letting Drew lead the way. He thought she kept back from him to avoid conversation. But, actually, it was out of fear. If he couldn't see her face, he wouldn't know how scared she was.

She'd always traveled with people of her own caliber and she certainly wasn't used to traveling like this. She'd heard how barbarous the Indians were and knew for a certainty that a red-skinned savage was lurking behind every rock and tree just waiting to scalp her. That was one of the reasons she was glad that Sinclair was along.

Not that he would be any protection to her with that silly little riding crop of his. But just being in the presence of a civilized man added a little support.

Dawn eventually broke over the horizon and a belt of red, pink, and orange separated the sky from the mountains, leaving her less frightened in the small amount of light. They'd been traveling steadily for two hours when Drew stopped in the shade of several oak trees.

Dismounting before Sinclair, Drew reached up to help Melissa down, his hands almost encircling her small waist. Placing her hands on his shoulders, their eyes met for a brief instant as he swung her to the ground.

"Are you all right, Melissa?" Sinclair asked, dismounting and hurrying to her.

"Of course, Charles," she answered demurely, smiling sweetly over at him and giving Drew a sideways glance, dusting her gloved hands together.

With his hands still tingling from the warm feel of her, Drew opened the food sack and handed them a piece of dried meat.

"Is this it?" she asked, her pink lips curling back slightly as she held the jerky gingerly in her fingers.

"My good man," Sinclair snorted, sniffing the meat, "I thought that you'd build a fire and cook something."

"If my father knew that I was being forced to eat this . . . this . . . " she complained, looking down disgustedly at the jerky. Then she asked, "What is this anyway?"

Just then a horrifying thought struck her and her eyes widened. The sick expression froze on her suddenly pale face. Raising her gaze slowly, she looked at Drew. Really looked at him. "Is this rattlesnake?" she asked through clenched teeth, starting to throw it down.

"No, no," Drew said quickly, grabbing her hand and wanting to laugh so badly he thought he'd burst. "It's only dried beef. It's good for you. Just bite off a small piece and chew until you can swallow. I promise I won't make you eat rattlesnake as long as we're traveling."

"Just when are we going to eat?" Sinclair wanted to know harshly, watching Melissa break off small pieces and chew. Following her example, Sinclair made a face as he tasted it.

"Around noon, I guess," Drew answered, retying the food sack. "Let's go," he continued, walking beside Melissa to help her mount.

Once they were traveling, Melissa lapsed into silence, riding a little closer to Drew. Pretending to look around for signs of trouble, he noticed that she was still breaking off the meat and chewing. Once their gazes met and he thought that she would smile. But she didn't. She just switched the parasol to her left shoulder and broke off another bite.

Drew glanced back at Sinclair and was stunned to see that the Englishman had taken a large white handkerchief and had wrapped it around his head to cover his ears and the back of his neck. But the narrow brim didn't do much to keep the sun from his face.

Without comment, Drew reached back into the saddle bag where he'd put the colonel's treasured hat and under their scrutiny removed it.

"Here, Sinclair," he said, handing him the hat, "this might keep the sun off your neck better. It might help if you turned your collar up, too." The fair skin exposed between the hair and shirt was already turning a bright pink.

"Thanks awfully, Williams," Sinclair said, taking off the small hat. Doing as he was told, he turned up his collar and put on the big flat-crowned hat. The contrast it made with his riding clothes and boots was a sight to behold.

Drew wondered if they were aware of the beautiful country around them. Purple mountains. Red rock formations almost touching the blue sky. Huge green cactus, with outreaching arms. Traveling in the country was a joy and pleasure to Drew. But they probably couldn't have cared less.

Drew felt sorry for Melissa. He wouldn't want to be in her position for anything. To be someone important enough for somebody else to want to harm just because of who she was.

He'd been shot at and hit several times during the war. Even since he'd been a scout, he'd been shot. But it wasn't because of who he was. It was because of his job.

They plodded along. The sun was up high now and beat down on them relentlessly. Sweat ran down their backs. Drew's blue shirt stuck to him and he saw that Melissa had unbuttoned her tight-fitting jacket. Sinclair was mopping his face with the white handkerchief.

"Miss Dunbar," Drew said, looking back at her, "you might be cooler if you take off your jacket." He was surprised when she did it. The long-sleeved white blouse fitted as tightly as the jacket and was damp enough to cling to her. Drew noticed how it clung to her high, firm bosom.

"Isn't that better?" he asked, smiling slightly at her.

"Yes. It is," she replied, the stony expression still on her face. "Thank you." She laid the jacket across her leg around the saddle horn and said no more.

"Sinclair, how are you doing back there?" Drew asked, turning around in the saddle.

"As well as can be expected under these adverse conditions, I expect," Sinclair answered, a civil tone in his voice, still mopping his face.

Few trees on the flat land offered little protection for the travelers. The rocks and ground seemed to catch the heat and throw it back at them in defiance. Frequently they took drinks of the tepid water from the canteens.

The first time Melissa drank from the canteen, she'd asked for a glass.

"How am I supposed to drink this?" she'd asked contemptuously, holding the brown container in her gloved hands.

"Unscrew the cap, put it to your mouth, and swallow," Drew instructed, hiding a smile behind his canteen.

Tipping her canteen back in the manner Drew did, the water rushed out and dribbled down her chin.

"Didn't you bring a glass?" she asked, her eyes blazing.

"No," Drew replied simply, taking several drinks and closing the canteen.

"Well, really," came the English voice. "This is the most uncivilized thing that I've ever seen," following Drew's example. "When my riding club was out in the country, we always carried a drinking glass."

"You've got the best drinking glass available," Drew replied. "You have the whole thing right there in your hand. No chance of dropping a glass and breaking it."

"Well, I certainly didn't expect such inconveniences," Melissa complained, dabbing her lips with a small yellow handkerchief. "You can rest assured that my father will hear about this."

"I only hope that you'll be able to tell him about this," Drew said mildly with a raised eyebrow.

"What do you mean?" she asked, a frown drawing her brows together.

"The Daytons are after you, you know," he told her, meeting her gaze. His heart skipped a beat as he looked at her. He'd never seen such beautiful eyes. They reminded him of a small fawn's eyes he'd seen once. Big, brown, and soft. Her eyes would probably be soft like the fawn's when she wasn't so mad.

"They're planning to kidnap you so your father won't sign that agreement with Chief Half Moon next week," he informed her, when he finally found his voice.

"Who are these Daytons you keep speaking of?" Sinclair asked, riding up by Drew's left side.

"The Daytons are three brothers: Cap, the oldest, Tom, the middle, and Slade, the youngest. They're called commancheros. They got in good with the Indians, giving them guns if they would rob wagon trains and settlements. The Indians divide their take with the Daytons and in return the Daytons kill the buffalo and ship the hides off."

"Then why would the Indians want to break with them and sign an agreement with the government?" Melissa asked, perplexed. She rode closer to him now hanging onto every word that he said.

"Because," Drew said, enjoying her attention, "the meat goes to waste. The carcasses are left to rot in the sun. The only things that benefit from the meat are buzzards and bugs. The Indians are finally getting tired of seeing the meat ruined and are willing to stop their dealings with the Daytons if the government will help them."

"Why do these men do this," Sinclair asked, "if they know that it robs the Indians of food?"

"I can tell you in one word," Drew replied in disgust. "Money! They get a good price for the hides."

"They wouldn't really kidnap me, would they?" Melissa asked, shaking her head, a smile beginning on her lips.

"Yes," Drew replied simply. He didn't want to spare her. He wanted her to know exactly what they were up against. He didn't know whether she believed him or not. But at least she'd been told. Apparently she did believe him, though, because he saw a shiver run through her as she licked her lips and swallowed.

One of the times they stopped, Drew poured water on a handkerchief and wiped the horses' noses and around their mouths.

"Why did you do that?" Melissa asked, watching him.

"Dust gets in their nose, Melissa," Sinclair explained patiently, surprising them both. "The dust makes breathing hard and slows the horses down. The riding club told us if we were ever in a dusty place, to take good care of the animals." Sinclair looked very pleased with himself when Drew nodded in agreement.

"We could go faster," she suggested, watching Drew from the corner of her eye.

"The horses would only get hot and we'd have to stop longer," Drew said. But he did urge the horses into a lope for a while, then slowed them down. No use wasting good animals on the whim of a spoiled woman.

Noon found them by one of the few watering places on the desert. A small stream with clean water reflected the blue sky. Yellow, red, and blue flowers dotted the area. Rocks, cactus, and palo verde added more beauty to this primitive land and there was green grass around the stream.

Hunger pangs gnawed at his stomach and Drew knew that his charges must be hungry, too, since they hadn't eaten in six hours.

Again Drew dismounted before Sinclair and helped Melissa down. He took the coffeepot and frying pan from his saddle bags. The three tin cups and plates made a clanking noise as he carried them to a log and put them down.

"Are we really going to eat?" Melissa asked sarcastically.

"Yes, we are," Drew replied in the same tone, building a small fire from pieces of wood that were scattered around. Walking toward the stream with the coffeepot, he handed Sinclair his pocket knife.

"There's a can of beans in the food sack," he said. Sinclair looked at him for a moment. But Drew didn't wait to see what he would do. He just turned on his heel and went on to the stream.

Returning, he was surprised to see that Sinclair had really opened the beans and that Melissa was stirring them in the pan. Drew put the pot on the fire and they sat down to wait for the coffee to make. Melissa, still using her own initiative, took the three plates and spooned the steaming beans into them passing the plates to the men.

They moved away from the fire to sit under the shade of an oak tree. Drew sat cross-legged on the ground. Sinclair dusted off a log near Drew, spread the handkerchief out, and he and Melissa sat down.

"Sinclair, I guess you're wishing that you were back in Philadelphia?" Drew said, sipping the strong coffee.

"Well, yes, as a matter of fact," the Englishman replied, "I am. I've read of this country. But I'd thought that it was just someone's imagination and they decided to write about it." He pushed the colonel's hat back on his head and chewed thoughtfully. "You mentioned the Daytons kidnapping Melissa. Isn't it your job to prevent such a thing from happening?

My job is to get Miss Dunbar to her father," Drew replied. "If preventing a kidnapping falls into that category, I'll do my best. By the way, Sinclair. Can you use a gun?"

"Of course," Sinclair replied, avoiding Drew's eyes while he sipped his coffee and frowned. "The members of my club are expert marksmen. But we never shot at another man."

"Well," Drew said, swallowing the coffee with gusto, "the Daytons are just a cut below humans and a cut above animals. So there should be no problem."

So far Melissa hadn't said anything. She just picked at the beans and took tiny sips of the coffee.

"Did you leave anyone in Philadelphia to pine in your absence, Miss Dunbar?" Drew asked, with a sideways glance, working up to the question. He wanted to know if she was romantically involved with anyone before he made a fool of himself.

"Mr. Williams," she said cooly, sliding her gaze toward him and for the first time calling him something, "your job is to get me safely to my father. Not to ask questions about my personal life. Which happens to be none of your business in the first place."

"Sorry," was the only comment Drew made and that in a flat voice. They finished eating in silence.

Drew finished eating first and stretched out flat on the ground, his arm under his head. Pulling his hat over his face, he dozed until he didn't hear the sound of their forks scraping against the tin plates.

Standing up, still without comment, he picked up his plate, took theirs without looking at Melissa, got the coffeepot and frying pan, and went to the stream to wash them. These put away in the saddle bags, he took the almost empty canteens to the stream. Just as he finished filling the last one, a nerve-splitting scream echoed through the canyons.

The Daytons! That was the first thing that popped into his mind. His heart almost stopped and a cold chill ran over him. Drew knew that Sinclair wouldn't shoot anyone even if he had a gun. He should have made them go with him. But it was only a short distance. If it had been the Daytons, Drew would have heard them. But there was always that possibility.

Jerking his gun from the holster, Drew raced back to them. Melissa was standing by the log, her hands framing her white face, her eyes wide in terror. Sinclair, clutching the riding crop in his right hand, was standing perfectly still.

"What's the matter?" Drew asked, looking around and seeing nothing out of the ordinary. Speechless, Melissa pointed a shaking finger toward the log where she and Sinclair had been sitting.

Coiled at the end of the log was a black and white bull snake. Shaking his head, Drew holstered his gun, bent down, picked up a rock, and threw it at the reptile that wiggled away into the rocks.

"Why didn't you kill it?" Melissa cried, glancing at him.

"There was no reason to," Drew said softly. "It wasn't poison. Besides, a shot can be heard for miles out here. If anyone is following us, they'd be sure to hear it."

"Well, really," Sinclair said imperiously, regaining his composure. "We've been traveling since before dawn. If someone is after us, we would certainly have seen them before now." He gave his boot a swat with the riding crop.

Drew's patience ran out just then. Here was a man getting smart with him about an impending matter and just a minute ago was afraid of a harmless snake.

"Sinclair," Drew said in an even tone but with an edge in it, "if you say 'well really' one more time, I'm going to take that riding crop and cram it down your throat. The Daytons aren't in a hurry. We're the ones pressed for time," Drew's blue eyes snapped and Sinclair knew he meant what he said. "You can believe me. The Daytons are out there."

Suddenly tears began rolling down Melissa's pale face and she sank to her knees on the ground, crying hysterically, sobs shaking her slender shoulders.

Sinclair made a step toward her. But Drew shook his head and Sinclair stopped. Drew also wanted to comfort her, but he decided it was best to leave her alone and let her cry it out. Sinclair turned an embarrassed red at being taken down by Drew in front of Melissa and at seeing a woman crying and walked away.

When she'd cried it out, Drew put his arm around her shoulders and helped her to her feet. Tears were still streaming down her cheeks and he handed her his bandanna to wipe her face.

"Are you all right?" he asked gently, taking her arm and leading her toward the horses.

"Yes," she replied in a quivering voice. "Mr. Williams," she said, taking a deep breath, making no attempt to mount. She looked up at him, tear drops on the tip of her long lashes, "I owe you an apology. I've been very rude to you since yesterday. I know you don't like this job and that you were made to take it. I'm very sorry for the way I've acted and Charles should apologize, too."

"Oh, there's no need to apologize, Miss Dunbar," Drew said, shrugging off her words, bewildered at the sudden change in her and wondering how long it would last. He bent down and boosted her up on the horse. "If I was in your place, I guess I'd do the same thing."

"It's just that I've never traveled like this before and it's hard for me to believe that there are men like the Daytons," she said, settling herself in the saddle and handing him his bandanna.

"Well, there are, and they're out there, Miss Dunbar," Drew said positively, putting the canteens on the horses. Sinclair was already mounted. He hadn't offered to help with anything.

"The Daytons are just waiting for the right time," Drew said, once they were moving. "Do you have a gun?" he asked, facing her. She was riding beside him now. Sinclair had dropped back behind them. Drew had seen no bulge to show that she carried a gun on her and the drawstring purse was too small to hold one. She looked at him with a raised eyebrow.

"Yes," she replied, giving him a captivating smile and turning pink. "I have a gun and if and when the time comes, you'll see it." She gave no hint to where she had one hidden.

"Sinclair," Drew called out, "just how good are you with a gun?"

"Well, re..." Sinclair began, but remembering what Drew had said about the riding crop, he hurriedly went on as he rode up by them. "A gentleman shouldn't have to use a gun to settle an argument. There are more civilized ways to handle things."

"All right," Drew said passively, drawing his mouth into a thin line, "when we meet the Daytons, I'll let you talk to them." Sinclair turned white and mopped his face again.

They rode steadily for two hours after lunch. A clump of palo verde offered a little shade, so they stopped to rest and drink more of the warm water from the canteens. This time Sinclair dismounted first and helped Melissa down.

"About two miles from here, past those rocks," Drew said, pointing westward, "is a way station. If trouble comes, it will happen before we reach it."

They were on a rise and stretching out below them was a valley. It looked so peaceful. But the survival of the fittest went on down there among the desert creatures just as it was up here where they were. Buzzards circled over some fallen animal as the cycle of life went on.

Sinclair was walking around, kicking his legs to get the kinks out. Melissa was looking off into the distance. Drew walked over to her, standing as close as he dared. Lilacs drifted on the wind again and it was all he could do to keep from reaching out and pushing back a strand of honey-colored hair from her face. He went so far as to take a step toward her.

To give his hands something to do, he took a pair of binoculars from the saddle bags and scanned the area. But he saw nothing out of the ordinary.

"What are we going to do," Sinclair asked, coming up beside them, "if those men are waiting for us."

"I really don't know," Drew replied earnestly, shaking his head. "We'll just have to wait and see what happens."

Melissa walked to her horse and the two

men almost fell over each other trying to beat the other to her. Drew stepped aside and watched amused as Sinclair tried to bend down, take her foot in his hand, and boost her up as he'd seen Drew do. But his foot turned under the added weight and he almost dropped her. Clinging to the saddle, she managed to pull up and settle herself in the saddle. Reproachfully she looked down at Sinclair.

"Charles, next time let Mr. Williams help me," she said irritably. "I don't want to arrive in Tucson with a broken neck." Sinclair uttered an oath under his breath and got on his horse.

As Drew had predicted, about a mile from where they'd stopped, they saw three men waiting on horses at the side of the trail.

"If they ask," Drew told them as they approached the men, "you're my wife Clara and we've only been married two weeks. Sinclair, you're her brother. I don't know if they've seen Senator Dunbar's daughter or a picture of her. But I'm sure they know her name."

"Williams," Sinclair asked, a set expression in his eyes, "how often does a stage come through here back to the fort?"

Both Drew and Melissa gaped at him as though they didn't believe what they were hearing.

"I've decided," Sinclair continued, dropping his gaze from theirs, mopping his face again with the handkerchief that was now grimy, "that I just can't take this any longer. I think it's best that I go back to the fort. I know that Melissa is in good hands and that you can get her to Tucson without any more help from me."

Drew stared at him, wondering what help he meant. If the situation hadn't been so grave, Drew would have laughed.

"Charles, you can't mean it," Melissa cried out, reaching over and taking his hand.

"Yes, I do," Sinclair insisted pensively. "I'm just not cut out for this." He mopped his face once more and turned to Drew. "I'm very sorry, Williams. I'll go along with anything you tell those men."

"Sinclair, you're making a mistake," Drew argued. He didn't really like Sinclair. But he didn't want to see the Englishman do something that could cost him his life. "What if the Daytons decide to wait at the way station? There may not be a stage for a good while. All kinds of things could happen."

"I'll hide somewhere," Sinclair said gruffly. "They won't find me. Besides, if there isn't a stage soon, I can get back to the fort alone."

"Charles," Melissa pleaded, "you could get lost. You haven't paid any more attention to directions than I have. We've been relying on Mr. Williams entirely."

"No, I won't," Sinclair persisted.

"Well, have it your own way," Drew said relenting, realizing that time was wasting.

"I hope you know what you're doing," Melissa said calmly to Drew with a raised eyebrow. "If anything happens to me, my father will have your hide."

"Miss Dunbar," Drew said patiently, "if anything happens to you, then it will have to happen to me first. If it does happen, there won't be enough hide to go around."

Melissa removed her gloves, putting them in her purse. Switching the parasol to her right shoulder, she moved her horse closer to Drew.

Reaching out, she took his right hand in hers. Drew never had anything to shock him so. Uncontrollably, his fingers closed tightly around hers. To the pure astonishment in his eyes, she said, "Well, if we're newly married, we might as well act like it."

"Has the stage passed through here yet?" Drew called out casually, very conscious of the small, warm hand in his as they approached the three men in dirty clothes and beards.

"No, not yet," the oldest-looking one said. Drew guessed that this was Cap. "We've been waitin' about half an hour."

Drew knew then that they thought Melissa would be on a stage and had planned to kidnap her before the stage reached the way station. It hadn't occurred to them that she could be traveling another way. But why would they be here today?'

The other men hadn't said anything. They just took in every inch of Melissa who sat on her horse as though she did this sort of thing every day.

"Where you folks headin'?" the man asked in a gravelly voice, scratching his dirty red beard thoughtfully.

"To Benson Wells," Drew answered, hoping the lie sounded convincing to them. It wasn't to him. Drew had never been one to lie about anything.

"Benson Wells, you say?" the man repeated, catching his under lip between yellow and broken teeth. "Who are you and who are they?"

The three men rode closer to them. Melissa recoiled, pulling her hand from Drew's as the rank smell of animals, dirty clothes, and sweat reached her nose. She let her horse move a few feet back. These men probably hadn't bathed in several weeks. The man who'd been talking stared intently at Melissa with a calculating look.

"I'm Drew Williams and this is my wife Clara. This is," Drew indicated over his shoulder with a nod of his head, "Charles Sinclair, her brother. Who are you and what business is it of yours who we are?" Drew looked Dayton straight in the eye, easing his right hand toward his pistol.

"I'm Cap Dayton and these are my brothers, Tom and Slade," Cap said. "It'll be a lot of our business if you're lyin'."

Cap removed his filthy hat and ran his fingers through his greasy red hair.

"How long you been married, little lady?" the one indicated as Slade asked, a surly grin on his pocked and thin face.

"Two weeks," Melissa replied, drawing her horse up by Drew again. He shot her a quick look, surprised that she could lie so quickly.

"How come you ain't wearin' a weddin' ring?" Tom asked, eyeing Melissa's hands, his brown eyes suspicious.

Drew wished that the marriage idea had occurred to him sooner. She should have been wearing a ring on her left hand. The pearl and diamond ring on her right hand wasn't the kind to be used for a wedding ring. He'd have to think of something fast.

"Well," Drew drawled, winking at Melissa as though they shared a secret, "you know how it is." He reached out, taking her hand again. "We decided to get married so fast that I didn't have time to buy her a ring. Her father, you know?"

"Hey, mister," Cap called out to Sinclair who'd been silent until now, "why are you so quiet?"

"I'm not feelin' so good," Sinclair said with an authentic-sounding Southern drawl. "The sun doesn't beat down like this in New Orleans."

Drew wondered how Sinclair knew about New Orleans, then guessed that Colonel Walters had talked to him about the place. Walters never missed an opportunity.

"That must be where you got them fancy clothes," Tom jeered.

Then they switched their attention back to Drew and Melissa, exchanging knowing looks and malicious smiles.

"Are you catchin' a stage for a honeymoon somewhere?" Slade asked, reaching over and slapping Tom on the back. Both men threw back their heads and roared with laughter.

"We are on our honeymoon and are going to Benson Wells to live," Melissa answered sharply, glaring at them.

"Well," Cap said slowly, scratching his beard again. "I guess you're who you say you are. You can go."

"Who are you waiting for way out here?" Drew asked innocently. "Why don't you go on to the way station? It would be a lot cooler."

"Oh, it's gonna be a surprise," Cap replied, grinning at his brothers. "We're gonna meet somebody on the stage and we don't want to go all the way to the station."

Dayton was lying. It was as plain as the filth on him. There were no houses out here and it would be pointless to meet a stage out in the middle of nowhere without some devious plan in mind.

Without pressing their luck, Drew, Melissa, and Sinclair moved their horses into a fast pace to give the impression that they didn't have too far to go and didn't mind spending them. But when they were out of the Daytons' sight, they slowed the horses down.

Reaching the way station, they stopped just long enough to bid farewell to Sinclair.

"Charles, I wish you'd change your mind," Melissa begged. "Those men will be looking for us and they'll find you."

"No, they won't," Sinclair said patiently, reaching across and kissing her on the cheek. "Williams," he said, extending his hand. Drew shook it, wondering if Sinclair could really make it back to Fort Rather alone.

Drew knew that a stage wouldn't be along for at least another hour and that hour would put them that much farther down the road. So without more delay, they left Sinclair there in the blazing sun.

"I hope he knows what he's doing," Drew

said when the way station was lost to view as they went over a hill.

"He seemed to be confident in Philadelphia and on the way out here," Melissa said sadly. "But when he saw the men wearing guns, he seemed to lose himself." Glancing around at the vastness, she continued, "This country didn't help matters much either."

As the afternoon dragged into evening and the shadows grew longer, Drew began giving thought to where they would spend the night. There were no houses or shacks where they could stay. He knew Melissa would throw a fit when he had to tell her that they'd have to sleep on the ground.

She didn't get as mad, though, as he thought she would. Her good mood was still holding. But she did look surprised, however. And he didn't blame her for that.

"On the ground?" she exclaimed wide-eyed, looking dubiously at the sand, rocks, and grass where they'd stopped under the sparse shade of trees. "With all those crawly things?"

"I've slept on the ground a lot of times," Drew told her, "and nothing ever got me."

"Maybe nothing wanted you," she said, smiling mischievously. "What will we sleep on or in?" she asked, looking frantically around her.

"Oh, we're lucky this time," he said, helping her down. "There're trees here and rocks. There's a good place for the bedrolls," he said, pointing to a level spot on the ground.

"I've never slept in a bed . . . roll . . . before,"

she said, hesitating over the term. She'd never discussed sleeping arrangements with a man other than her father before.

"I imagine you're going to do a lot of things on this trip that you've never done before," Drew said, spreading the blankets on the ground. He handed her the dress and she put it, with her jacket, under the saddle.

"Won't it be cold on the ground?" she asked, standing beside him, looking uncertain.

"No," he answered, standing up. "You sleep on one blanket and cover with the other. When you get a place warm on the ground, it'll stay warm."

Turning his back so he wouldn't embarrass her too much, he said, "You can go behind those rocks if you want to undo or unlace something. It'll be safe there."

He heard her gasp for breath. But when he turned around, she was gone.

"We'll have a cold supper," he said on her return.

"Why?" she asked, sitting down on the blanket.

"Well," he explained, "I guess the Daytons have discovered by now that we didn't get on any stage and that Melissa Dunbar wasn't on a stage. If we make a fire and they see it, we'll have more trouble than we can handle in the dark."

Opening the food sack, he handed her a piece of dried meat and opened a can of beans. Without comment, she ate and even offered to wash the dishes when they'd finished.

"We don't have enough water," Drew told

her. "I'll just rub sand in them and when we get to a river or stream, I'll wash them." He knew she didn't like the idea of cleaning with sand by the way she looked at him, with her head lowered and raised eyebrows. That's why he added the part about the river.

"I wonder how Charles is doing?" she asked plaintively. "I thought that he would have more courage than he did. He was always talking about that courageous riding club of his in England." She sounded so contemptuous that Drew was glad she wasn't talking about him.

"Oh, I wouldn't be too hard on him," Drew said, thinking about the arrogant young man. "It took a lot of guts to wait back there. I imagine he can take care of himself." Drew wasn't too sure about that and said it only for her peace of mind.

Darkness came over the desert, bringing the cold night air. Melissa lay down and pulled the blanket over her. Drew sat awake for a long time, listening to the sounds of the night.

The mournful sounds of a coyote hung on the night air. The moon whitewashed the desert with its light and an owl asked its question. Crickets sang their song and the night birds joined in. Drew glanced at Melissa, glad to see that she was asleep. He could hear her even breathing and knew that she must be exhausted.

He didn't know how long he'd been asleep when he felt a hand on his shoulder. With quick and trained reflexes, he reached out and grabbed the arm. He let go when he heard

Melissa whisper, "It's me," close to his ear. Her hair had come loose and brushed his face. In the moonlight, he could plainly see her face. Fear was mirrored in her big brown eyes.

"What's the matter?" he asked in a whisper, covering her trembling hand with his, drawing his gun with the other.

"I heard a noise," she whispered, turning her hand over under his and clutching his fingers. A faint fragrance of lilacs hovered around her as she moved closer to him.

He listened intently for a moment. There was definitely something there. Something moving in the bushes. But if it was the Daytons, they would have already been on them. Their horses would have made more noise than that. The horses from the fort were standing still.

"It's probably just a wolf or a coyote," Drew said softly to reassure her.

"Are they dangerous?" she asked, sitting down close to him on his blanket.

"It depends on how hungry they are," he teased, smiling to himself, liking the feel of her so close to him.

"I hope these aren't very hungry," she said in a shaky voice, making no attempt to move. In fact, she moved closer, still holding on to his hand.

Just then an armadillo appeared in the moonlight and quickly scurried into a clump of bushes.

"What in the world was that?" Melissa asked, expelling the breath she'd been holding.

"Only an armadillo," he said with a catch in his voice.

"Only an armadillo?" she repeated. "Doesn't anything ever bother you?"

"Yes," he said, looking deep into her eyes, clearing his throat, still conscious of her so close to him and her perfume like a veil around them and her hand in his. "Every now and then something bothers me."

She looked searchingly at him for a moment. Then she pulled her hand from his and stood up.

"Well, that takes care of that," she said, going back to her blanket.

Drew sat awake for a while after Melissa had gone back to sleep. He didn't understand this new feeling that made his mouth dry and his hands sweat and his heart beat frantically. But he did know that he liked it.

Finally, with a silly smile on his face, he stretched out again and went to sleep.

Chapter Three

Drew awoke the next morning just as the sun was peeping over the purple mountains. He'd never slept this late before and was angry with himself. The Daytons would have a head start on them!

Sitting up, Drew rubbed the sleep from his eyes and pushed his hair back from his face. Glancing at Melissa, he saw that she was still sleeping soundly. Knowing that she must be bone tired, Drew didn't mind too much that they'd overslept.

Tousled honey-colored hair covered half of her face as she lay on her side. Black lashes fluttered on her fair cheek that was a little blistered from the sun and wind yesterday. Her chest rose and fell in slow and even breathing. Drew sat there for a moment taking in the sight of her. Never before had he seen a woman so pretty. He could still feel her hand in his and her hand on his arm from last night when she'd been frightened.

But time was wasting and he couldn't sit there looking at her all day. Not with the Daytons breathing down their necks. Drew knew that they were certainly being followed now. Cap Dayton wasn't the kind of man who'd let anybody make a fool out of him and get away with it.

Getting up with the agility of a cat, being used to sleeping anywhere, Drew stepped over to Melissa. He had to call her several times before she opened one eye and pushed her hair back.

"It's time to get up," he said cheerfully, smiling down at her. She started to sit up, but her sore muscles and aching bones rebelled and she fell back on the blankets, her eyes shut tightly. Catching her breath and her under lip between her teeth, she lay tense almost struggling for breath.

"Need some help?" Drew asked, seeing the tortured look on her face. She nodded without trying to hide the pain in her eyes. Bending down and with his arm around her shoulders, Drew tried to help her up. Her face grimaced in agony as she struggled to her feet still holding on his arm, her fingers digging in. He saw her face turn white and felt a tremble run through her as she began rising from the ground.

"Oh, easy," she wailed, catching her breath again, finally standing up straight and gripping his arm to steady herself.

"How did you sleep?" he asked, turning her loose and walking toward the horses and throwing the saddles on them.

"Not too bad," she replied, just standing there. "You were right about the ground being warm." A slight smile brightened her face as she began moving slowly. "I guess we'll have a cold breakfast?"

"You guessed it," he said, smiling at her over his shoulder as he tightened the cinch on his horse. "But one good thing about it. We'll be moving."

She walked slowly and stiffly behind the rocks to redo whatever it was that she'd undone last night. When she returned, her hair was combed back from her face and tied with a green ribbon that matched her dress and hat, and her face had a clean, washed look. Then he noticed that she'd taken one of the canteens that she stood holding out to him.

"I can't do a thing with a dirty face and hands," she said. "I hope that I didn't use too much water." This was more of an explanation than an apology. There was no malice in her voice. She was just stating a fact.

"There's a creek about a mile from here where we can water the horses and refill the canteens," he said.

"Why didn't we go there last night?" she asked, looking up at him in bewilderment as they stood by her horse.

"Because it would have been too dark by the time we got there," he explained, bending down to take her foot in his hand. He straightened up when she didn't move. She just shook her head.

"I don't think that I can make it," she said dejectedly. "My bones refuse to move that much. I guess I'll just have to walk to Tucson." Both of them laughed until tears glistened in their eyes. But time was wasting. Putting his hands around her waist, Drew lifted her up. Getting her left foot into the stirrup wasn't too difficult. But when she tried to raise her right leg and wrap it around the saddle horn, that was different. She turned white again and Drew thought she'd faint.

"Oh!" she moaned, reaching over and grabbing her right knee frantically in both hands.

The motion threw her sideways causing her to fall from the saddle. Some previous training made her jerk her left foot from the stirrup, which was a good thing, because the spirited horse shied away and trotted a few paces. If Drew hadn't been there to catch her, she would have landed on the ground.

Drew felt his heart turn over in his chest and slam against his rib as he stood there holding her in his arms, clasping her tightly against his chest. She was a lot lighter than he thought she would be and he held her tighter. Her hair brushed against his face and the fragrance of lilacs came to him again.

When she'd felt herself falling, she'd thrown her left arm around his neck. Her right hand still clutched her knee. But as he tightened his arms around her and held her, she put the other arm around him.

Their eyes met and held in a long look. Hers big and questioning. His blue and steady. A pink blush crept up her face. Then still holding her close to him, he stood her down. "I'll get the horse," he said huskily. She only nodded her head and Drew walked away.

Catching the horse, Drew led it back to where she was still standing. This time he picked her up bodily, one arm around her shoulders, the other under her legs and placed her on the saddle.

Once again she got her left foot into the stirrup and began rubbing her right knee gently as she eased it around the saddle horn.

"Are you all right?" Drew asked, seeing the color drain from her face again, really concerned that she was so sore.

"I'm all right," she said through clenched teeth, "if you can call bones and muscles that just don't want to work all right. I don't think that I've ever been or will ever be this sore again."

"I thought you said you rode a horse in Philadelphia regularly," Drew challenged, looking up at her.

"Oh, I haven't been on a horse in over a year," she confessed, avoiding his eyes.

"Well, we only have two more days to go," Drew said, smiling mischievously up at her as he stood by the horse.

"Two more days," she moaned, still rubbing her knee that she'd finally gotten around the saddle horn. "I only hope my body lasts that long." Drew chuckled to himself as he got on his horse still feeling the warmth of her in his arms.

The morning was cool and the blue sky was dotted with a few fluffy white clouds that moved along slowly as though some invisible hand was giving them a gentle push.

The horses were well rested and Drew and Melissa rode a little faster. Drew knew that the Daytons should really be behind them now.

Drew tried to put himself in Cap Dayton's place. If someone had made a fool out of me like we undoubtedly did the Daytons, Drew thought to himself, I'd probable kill them the first chance I had and I'd forget about kidnapping.

The short hairs on the back of his neck felt as though they were standing out like waving flags. He kept glancing over his shoulder, expecting to see the three men just behind them.

But there was nothing. Absolutely nothing. There wasn't any dust behind them to indicate that they were being followed. All that he could see was cactus, sage bush, clumps of chaparral, and more of the endless mountains as far as the eye could see.

"Are you scared?" Drew asked Melissa when they'd reached the creek that he'd mentioned earlier.

"No," she answered, smiling at him as he helped her down. She held to his arm until she could stand straight by herself. "Colonel Walters told Charles Sinclair and me that you were the best man for this kind of job. So why should I be afraid? My life is in your hands."

Drew couldn't tell if she was being truthful or sarcastic when she said that she wasn't scared. He was still glad, though, that she was as congenial as she'd been yesterday.

He took the canteens from the saddles and led the horses to the stream for water, completely forgetting the dishes they'd used the night before. When he returned, she asked,

"Didn't you forget to wash the dishes?"

For a moment he stared at her, not knowing what she was talking about. Then he remembered. That's probably just like all women, he thought, they always remember things that really don't amount to a thing. He was accustomed to eating from sand-cleaned plates.

Drew hadn't been around women too much in his young life and he didn't understand their ways. Sometimes it seemed to him that he'd been a scout all of his life. He was in the Confederate army for two years under Lee. When the war was finally over, he drifted west, since his parents had died, and he had no one else. He didn't encounter many women and the ones he did meet were either too young, married, or were barroom girls. He wasn't the kind to fool around with married women and there was no use in getting tangled up with a barroom girl.

He'd rather know headstrong women like Melissa Dunbar. She was just spoiled and tried to see how far she could bully people. But that had come, so far he hoped, to an end.

With a grin that Melissa didn't understand, he took the plates from the saddle bags and handed them to her.

"I think you need a little exercise, so why don't you go wash them?" he suggested, thrusting the plates into her hands, watching her draw in her breath and her eyes widen. Then her expression softened and she turned and went to the stream.

Slowly she bent down and washed the plates and with both hands on her left knee she pushed herself up and limped back. He helped her up on the horse and watched as she eased her right leg around the saddle horn.

"Would you like me to rub your knee?" Drew asked, looking up at her, a noncommittal expression on his tanned face.

"No! I certainly would not," she snapped, her brown eyes blazing. A blush spread across her face. She didn't know whether or not he was joking.

"Just a suggestion," he said, shrugging and swinging up on his horse.

Drew noticed several times that she was actually looking around and really seeing the country. He was wondering if she was looking at the country or trying to see if there was anybody following them. He found out when he saw her looking down intently at the dry, parched ground as they rode along.

"Does it ever rain out here?" she asked, wiping the perspiration from her face with a small white handkerchief that she'd taken from the small purse.

"Every now and then," he said, pushing his hat back on his head. But the sun was too bright and he pulled it back down over his eyes. Melissa had the frilly parasol unfurled and it was keeping the sun from her face and neck better than he had expected. The little hat was perched on top of her honey-colored hair the same as it had been yesterday. She had her gloves on and the tops of them were tucked up under the cuffs of her blouse sleeves. She'd left her jacket off, rolled up with her extra dress.

"It doesn't rain very often, though," he continued. "It usually rains and snows in the winter. If it rains too much in the summer, there are usually flash floods."

"Flash floods?" she asked, frowning. "Why? What are flash floods?"

"Well, the rain is usually so hard and the ground so dry and baked," he explained, "that it doesn't seep into the ground fast enough. It has to go somewhere and you have a flash flood."

Drew had been wondering how and why the Daytons had met that particular stage. But he didn't want to take the chance of upsetting Melissa by mentioning it to her and make her think that someone was plotting against them at the fort. It could have been coincidence.

But then as though she'd read his mind, Melissa asked, "Have you given any thought as to why the Daytons met that stage yesterday?" A worried frown puckered her forehead and her face looked pinched.

"It has occurred to me," Drew confessed, "and the only explanation I have is that there is only one stage a day, so maybe they've been meeting a stage every day until the right one comes along."

"But how did they know that I was coming out here at all?" she asked, switching the parasol to her right shoulder.

"Now that I really don't know," Drew answered truthfully. "All Walters told me was to get you to Tucson because the Daytons were going to kidnap you if your father signed that agreement with Half Moon."

They had come out of a canyon and topped a rise that offered a view for miles around. Taking the binoculars from his saddle bags, he scanned the area. He still didn't see any dust clouds behind them. Their own horses had been kicking up enough dust to choke an army and three horses would surely be making more dust than they were.

Wonder where they are? he asked himself. I know they're there. They wouldn't give up so easily. A different expression must have marked his face because Melissa asked, "What's the matter?"

"Nothing," he answered, shaking his head. "That's just it. There's nothing out there. I've checked several times and there's no sign of the Daytons anywhere. They've got to be behind us somewhere, though. They wouldn't just quit."

"I wonder what Charles is doing?" Melissa asked, stretching her right leg out along the side of the horse's neck and rubbing her knee. "Do you suppose they found him and would hold him for ransom instead of trying to find me?"

"No," Drew answered, shaking his head slowly. "Sinclair isn't that important to your father." A stricken look crossed Melissa's face and he hurriedly continued, "Oh, he's important to your father in one sense. But Senator Dunbar wouldn't give up signing an agreement this important for him."

They rode several miles further and once again he checked for signs. The only thing he could see this time was dark clouds building up in the west. Of all times for a storm to be coming up, he complained silently.

Drew swept the glasses around again. This time for some kind of protection from the advancing rain. A small shack came into focus and it seemed to be only half a mile away.

Thunder rolled through the mountains and canyons, sounding like a giant being rudely awakened. Lightning threw its jagged finger through and across the sky like a yellow knife. Drew could see the gray of falling rain and it was moving steadily toward them.

"I guess our talking about a rain scared one up," he told her pointing toward the west. "Do you want to see?" She nodded and he handed her the glasses. Taking them, her fingers touched his. The touch didn't seem to bother her as she raised the glasses to her eyes.

"You know?" she said, taking them down, "it's almost beautiful. The black clouds against the blue sky and the red rocks and purple mountains." There was an expression of awe in her brown eyes and a genuine smile on her lips.

Taking the glasses from her, he put them back in the saddle bags. "It's pretty out here just about all of the time. But if we don't get somewhere in a hurry, we won't look so good. Come on. If we're lucky, we can make that shack before the rain gets here."

Kicking their horses in the side, they began the mad rush in a dead run down the hill toward the shack.

But their luck didn't hold. Huge drops of

rain pelted them as they raced down the hill. Then the sky really unloaded and the rain came down so hard that they could hardly see. Thunder banged around them like a drum and the lightning split the sky.

Drew glanced at Melissa through the pouring rain as they urged the horses faster. It was all he could do to keep from laughing at her. The green feather that had curled so fashionably across the front of her hat was drooping limply between her eyes, and her honey-colored hair, which had been tied so carefully, was dangling in wet strands around her face. The full skirt hung in heavy wet folds against her legs and her blouse was plastered to her revealing every line of her body. The frilly parasol was a complete disaster. It was beyond protection and repair and in disgust she threw it to the ground.

If Drew could have seen himself, he would have known that he didn't look any better than she did. Rain dripped from the brim of his hat and his own clothes were stuck to him.

Urging their horses to the limit of their endurance, they reached the shack as the deluge continued harder.

The shack was in much better condition than Drew had thought when he first saw it through the glasses. A slanted shingled roof topped the building and Drew guessed from the front doors that it had two rooms.

Pulling the horses to a halt, Drew jumped down and rushed around to help Melissa dismount, almost dragging her from the saddle.

The heavy weight of the wet skirt threw her against him and he kept his arm around her as they hit the door and staggered inside.

When they had wiped the rain from their eyes, Drew opened the door leading into the other room. He was surprised to find a dirt floor in there. Each room had a door leading outside and each room had two windows with shutters held in place with rusty hinges.

In the floored room was a small black potbellied stove with its pipe running out through the top of the roof. A small table with two chairs, a log bench sitting against the wall by the door, and a meager stack of wood in the corner completed the furnishings.

The rain still ran down the slanted roof of the shack in torrents. Ordinarily the horses would have been left outside after they'd been unsaddled. But since there was a dirt floor in the other room, Drew decided that there was no use in letting the room go to waste.

Opening the door from one room to the other, he unlatched the outside door of the dirt-floored room and dashed out into the pouring rain. Grabbing the horses' reins, Drew pulled them in. He unsaddled them and went into the next room, putting a chair against the door.

Melissa was standing in the middle of the room as though she didn't know what to do with herself. She had taken off the ruined hat and was squeezing water from her soaked hair.

"Did you put those horses in there?" she

asked, jerking around when she heard him close the door and a horse snort.

"Sure," Drew replied, taking off his hat and slinging water from it. "Why?"

"Do you expect me to share a house with horses?" she asked, the old tone creeping back into her voice, her eyes blazing.

With an indifferent shrug, he said, "If you don't want to stay in here, you can sleep outside. There was no use in letting those horses drown when they can be inside. Besides, if the horses don't mind staying in here with you, why should you mind staying in here with them?"

"Well, I'm certainly not going out there in all of that," she said with a wave of a wet arm toward the window where the rain could still be seen pouring down.

"You'd better get out of those wet clothes," he said, working at the stove, getting a fire going. Soon heat began to fill the damp room.

"I don't have anything to put on except the extra dress in the bedroll and I was saving that," she said, a disdainful look in her brown eyes.

"I'll fix that," Drew said, rubbing his hands together once more over the stove before going to the other room.

Taking the shirt, pants, and hat he'd bought from Tag out of the saddle bags, he stuck his head around the door, held the clothes out to her, and told her to put them on.

"Are they yours?" she asked skeptically, slowly taking the garments from him and unfolding them.

"No," he answered with a grin, "they're not mine. Now get them on before you get pneumonia."

Closing the door, he took his extra clothes from the other bag and changed, laying his wet things around to dry.

"Are you dressed yet?" he called out. But either she couldn't hear him over the noise of the pouring rain or she was ignoring him and having trouble getting her wet things off and the pants and shirt on.

He waited a few minutes longer, giving her a little more time, then he called out again.

"I'm as dressed as I'll ever be," she answered in an uncertain tone of voice. Drew couldn't imagine what could cause her to sound like something was caught in her throat.

Hurriedly opening the door, he stopped dead in his tracks, one hand on the door knob and the other on his gun.

Melissa stood before the stove in Tag's old clothes. If Drew had been able to conjure up a picture of her in those clothes while he was buying them from Tag two days ago, that picture would have been nothing like this.

She looked entirely different in the garments. If Drew hadn't known that they were the ones he'd bought from Tag, he would have sworn that someone had switched them on him.

The faded blue pants fitted snuggly across her hips and clung to her shapely legs all the way down to her small bare feet, whereas they had hung on Tag. If he hadn't always worn a belt through the loops, he would have lost them. But there was no way that Melissa could lose them.

The brown shirt had never been so well filled since the day it had been made. Especially the pockets. Melissa wasn't as tall as Tag, but she weighed a little more than he did and had more flesh on her bones in all the right places. The collar was open and the buttons strained as though they would pop with the next breath. There wasn't a wrinkle anywhere in the garment.

Drew knew that he just couldn't stand there staring at her for the rest of the day, although he would have liked to. So swallowing the lump in his throat, he said, "Tag would certainly be proud of those old clothes now."

"Tag?" she asked, spinning around at the sound of his voice. "Who's Tag?" she asked baffled and with raised eyebrows at the expression on his face.

"Tag Cooper is the boy who mends the saddles and bridles at the fort. He was the only one small enough whose clothes would fit you. I knew there would probably be some kind of situation where you would need to change and I bought them for you."

"How much did you pay for them?" she asked, taking a step toward her purse.

"I don't want any payment for them," he said, holding up his hand to ward off her intentions. Just seeing her in them was worth the price.

"Okay. I won't pay you for them," she said, "but I still want to know what they cost you."

"A whole dollar," he answered, smiling at her from across the room.

"A whole dollar," she repeated and laughed with the sound of bells ringing. "Would you believe that I've never worn anything that cost a dollar?"

"Well, there's a first time for anything," he told her. "You should laugh more often," he said, walking to the stove, holding his hands over it. He noticed that they were shaking.

"I would have never thought that a man would be buying me, a senator's daughter, an old pair of pants and a shirt," she said, smiling and combing her long hair out and back from her face with a small gold comb.

"Ma'am," he said, finding it hard to believe that this young woman, standing there in someone else's clothes, was the same headstrong person of yesterday, "a senator's daughter is no different from an Indian princess or a Cajun queen. They all get wet."

He put another log in the stove and glanced down at her bare feet.

"Where are your shoes?" he asked, frowning at her.

"Over there," she replied, pointing to a corner where she'd put her wet dress and petticoats on the log bench.

Drew walked to the shoes, picked them and a chair up, and brought them back to the stove.

"You'd better put your shoes on and let them dry on your feet so they won't shrink," he said. "Sit down and I'll help you."

Obediently she sat down in the rickety

chair and Drew went down on one knee. She had taken off her stockings and it was hard to slip her bare feet into the damp shoes. Her long skirt had kept a lot of the water off them and they weren't really all that wet.

Drew had only been emotionally involved with one girl before and couldn't understand exactly why his hands trembled so as he held Melissa's slender foot in his hand and worked with the tiny buttons. In any event, he was glad when the shoes were on. Glancing up at her, his heart caught in his throat. Her eyes met his and a pink blush covered her face. "Thank you," she murmured in a soft voice. He cleared his throat and stood up.

There were no lamps in the shack, so they made supper while there was still enough light to see. Melissa made coffee as she'd seen Drew do yesterday, while he was making flat bread. When the bread was done, he put it in one of the tin plates and opened a can of beans, emptying them into the same skillet in which he'd made the bread. He poured a cup of coffee, handed it to her, and she sipped it while the beans heated.

"I just thought of something," she said, putting down the cup of hot coffee, a worried look in her eyes, watching him intently.

"What?" Drew asked, looking up from his plate with no idea what she had in mind.

"Did it occur to you that those Dayton men could have been waiting here for us?" she asked, cupping her hands around the tin cup.

"No," he answered, breaking off a piece of bread. "We've been ahead of them all the way. We would have seen dust clouds behind us and unless the horses were put on the west side of the shack, I would have seen them through the glasses before getting here."

"Oh," she said with a smile, feeling childish in her worry. "But I still wonder how they knew which stage to meet."

"I really can't say," Drew told her, downing the last of his coffee.

After they'd finished eating, Drew went into the next room to check on the horses. He heard the door open and shut and couldn't imagine why Melissa would be opening the door with the rain coming down so hard. Surely she wasn't going outside.

The Daytons! Drew's heart almost stopped as the thought popped into his mind. Maybe the Daytons had finally caught up with them and were in the other room. But Melissa would have screamed. Maybe she couldn't scream!

Drawing his gun, Drew slipped quietly over to the door and opened it just a crack. Glancing around the room, he saw that nothing was missing and nothing extra was there.

Then he saw the coffeepot on the table. It was turned upside down on the table as though to drain.

Holstering his gun, he hurried into the room. Looking at the coffeepot again, he asked, "What did you open the door for? Did you hear something out there?"

"No, I didn't hear anything," she replied simply, wiping her hands on a handkerchief. "I was just emptying the coffeepot out. It's there on the table draining." She pointed over to the table and stood smiling at him as though waiting for him to compliment her on her thoughtfulness.

"You emptied the coffepot?" he asked slowly, staring at her.

She nodded in answer to his question. Then she frowned at the serious look in his eyes and wondered why he was making such an issue over something as simple as a coffeepot. "Shouldn't I have?"

"No," he snapped, shaking his head. "When you're out like this, you don't waste anything. That would have been enough coffee for breakfast."

Melissa looked at Drew for a minute, her eyes holding his. Then her face crumpled and she began crying.

"I was only trying to help," she sobbed. Her tears were Drew's undoing. Putting his arms around her, he pulled her close to him without any resistance and pressed her head against his chest with his left hand.

"When you get to Tucson, everything will be all right," he whispered against her hair and patted her on the back as though she were a child. Sobs shook her slender body and his shirt was soon wet from her tears. "Things are pretty much the same in Tucson as they are in Philadelphia," he continued. She felt soft and warm under his hands and he wished the moment could last.

Finally, and all too soon for him, her sobs subsided and he released her. She walked over to the stove and with her fingers wiped away the tears that streaked her face.

"I'm sorry I threw the coffee out," she said, sniffling.

"That's all right," Drew replied, still feeling the warmth of her in his arms. "Don't worry about it. It's just that I heard the door open and thought that the Daytons had gotten the drop on us."

It was almost dark now. If it hadn't been raining so hard, there would have been at least another hour of light. But the rain seemed to close in around the shack and its occupants like a blanket that had been draped over them. Drew opened the door in front of the small stove for more light.

The logs spat and sputtered as they burned into and dropped onto the others. The crackling fire and warmth created a relaxing atmosphere.

Drew, sitting in front of the stove, stretched his long legs out in front of him, crossing his feet at the ankles.

Melissa was moving around the room, picking up the plates, cups, and other utensils and washing them. Then she stacked them on the table, ready for morning.

Drew let his mind wander to a time further on with them in a better house and her puttering around the kitchen and him sitting in front of a fireplace. Supper would be over and they would sit and talk about husband and wife things.

"You'd better get the bedrolls," she said, bringing him back to the present.

That's probably like a woman, too, he thought, getting up. They nag you whether you're married to them or not. Going into the next room, Drew checked on the horses and got the bedrolls. He put the one that Melissa had used last night between the stove and wall. There would be more warmth there.

As he spread his blankets on the opposite side of the room by the door, Melissa stood watching him in silence.

"This may sound silly after all that we've been through together so far," she finally said when he'd sat down on the blanket and pulled off his boots that were now dry, "but am I supposed to sleep in here with you?" A blush crept up her face until it was lost in her hair.

"Unless you want to sleep in the other room with the horses or outside in the rain," he said, stretching out on the blanket and pulling the other one over him. "I'll admit that it is more confining than last night. But as tired as I am, you don't have a thing to worry about."

He heard her gasp in absolute shock. He knew that she wasn't used to being talked to like this. He closed his eyes, but she could see an amused smile on his lips.

For a minute she stood looking down at him. Then shaking her head furiously, she turned and walked behind the stove and sat down on her blanket with her back to the wall.

Sitting there like that for a while, she thought about the easy life she'd been used to all of these years. Now here she was, with a man she didn't know, sitting in a two-room shack with horses in one of the rooms and she in clothes that had been bought for her and had belonged to and been worn by someone else.

Usually her clothes were specially made for her by one of the best seamstresses in Philadelphia and she was always the one who'd given her old clothes away. But clothes didn't seem very important to her right now.

The uppermost thought in her mind was that there were three men following them who were intent upon kidnapping her. She was sure from what Drew had said, that if things didn't go their way, the Daytons would kill her.

Chills ran over her body as she thought about those dirty men that she'd seen yesterday. She shivered again even though it was nice and warm there by the stove. Melissa couldn't imagine them putting their dirty hands on her. Nausea swept over her as she remembered the stench and filth of the men.

She had twice felt Drew's arms around her and his hands on her waist countless times as he'd helped her up and down from the horse these past two days—and she hadn't minded at all. In fact, she'd liked it. But those men with their old filthy clothes and dirty hands!

Usually when kidnappers killed their victims, it was so they couldn't identify their captors, she told herself. But we all know these men, she reflected. My father knows them. Colonel Walters knows them. Even Charles Sinclair knows them.

Surely they wouldn't kill me, she thought, trying to reassure herself. Suddenly she wanted the reassurance of the sound of Drew's voice.

It was too quiet in the shack. The crackling of the fire just wasn't enough. She knew that he was tired and needed his rest, that he had more to worry about than she did. But she had to talk to him.

"Those men wouldn't kill me, would they?" she called out to him in the darkness.

Drew must have been wide awake because he answered her question immediately.

"Yes," he said simply. "If that was the only way they could keep your father from signing the agreement with Half Moon, they'd kill you in a minute."

"Why do you always have to tell the truth when I ask you a question?" she asked, a lightness in her voice.

"Hadn't you rather know the truth and be prepared for it than to find out that I had lied to you just to spare your feelings?" he asked.

"I suppose you're right," she said, feeling childish. I guess, she thought to herself, I'm just being silly.

Finally, in fatigue she eased her still aching body down on the rough blankets instead of the fine linen sheets that she was used to. Her eyelids became heavy and the steady sounds of the rain on the roof lulled her off to sleep.

Sometime during the night, Drew was awakened by the sounds of the horses moving restlessly around in the other room. Getting up quietly, he pulled his boots on, opened the door, and stepped outside. He was glad to see that the rain had stopped. He'd thought that as hard as it had been coming down, especially out here on the desert, it would last at least up in the day and that would have meant a loss of time.

He opened the door to the dirt-floored room from the outside, led the horses out, and hobbled them.

Then he stood listening to the sounds of the desert. Off in the distance a coyote bayed at the moon in the now cloudless sky where stars twinkled like so many candles. The air had a fresh and clean, washed smell and there was a cool crispness in the breeze. Drew took a deep breath, filling his lungs with the freshness.

Shutting the door as quietly as he could behind him, he peeped around the stove at Melissa. She was sleeping soundly but uncovered. There was a chill in the air, so Drew put another log in the stove and bent down to pull the blanket up over her. At his touch, she sprang awake, fright in her eyes at not remembering where she was. Then she did remember, recognized him, and smiled sleepily up at him.

Then for no reason, other than that she was a beautiful woman and he was a man, and it surprised him when he did it, he leaned down and kissed her lightly on the mouth.

Her lips were cool under his and didn't respond to the caress. But she didn't do anything drastic like slap his face as he had expected her to do. He straightened up and went back to his blankets on the other side of the room. He sat down and was about to pull his boots off and lie down.

"Have you known many Indian princesses and Cajun queens?" she asked, her voice coming to him soft and hesitant through the shadows cast by the fire in the stove.

"Now I could answer that question the way you did the other day, yesterday, in fact, and tell you that it's none of your business," he said without expression in his voice. "Why do you want to know?"

"Oh, for no reason really, I guess," she lied in a soft voice. But it pained her to think of him with another woman. "I was just wondering how many Indian and Cajun girls you've been out with in the rain and shared a cabin with horses."

He couldn't see her face. But if she looked as funny as she sounded, he was glad that it was dark because he would have laughed at her. She sounded like a young, teenaged girl trying to sound out a boy's feelings for her.

"How many men and horses have you shared a cabin with in your lifetime?" he asked, knowing it was an unfair question. But her question had been just as unfair to him.

Hearing her draw in a breath of indignation, he turned on his side away from her to go back to sleep.

He grinned as he heard her flouncing around and then she was still. But she wasn't asleep. She lay there thinking about his kiss. I wonder if he would have kissed me if Charles Sinclair had been here? she asked herself.

If he had wanted to, he probably would have. She smiled a little. He needed a shave, though. The light brown beard that had grown since yesterday had scratched her face and she raised her hand up and rubbed her cheek. She lightly touched her lips that were now warm with her fingers. But then a warmth had spread throughout her body. A feeling that no one else had been able to create in her.

This may be unladylike, she told herself, still feeling the touch of his lips on hers, but I'm glad Charles decided to go back to the fort.

"Well, for what's it's worth to you," she called out, "there's no one in Philadelphia to pine in my absence."

With a smile and her fingers on her lips again, Melissa turned over on her side and went back to sleep.

Chapter Four

As usual Drew was awake early the next morning. Through the small and grimy window in the front of the cabin, he could see the gray dawn breaking over the mountains. The morning air was cold and there was a chill in the cabin.

Stretching as he sat up, Drew looked over at Melissa. She was still sleeping soundly, the blanket pulled up tight around her neck.

Pulling on his boots and lacing them, he wondered what she'd thought about his kissing her last night.

He knew what he thought about it. He liked it. She probably thinks, though, he told himself as he sat there on the blankets, that she'll never see me again. That's probably why she didn't do or say anything.

Wanting to let her sleep as long as possible, Drew tiptoed quietly to the door and stepped outside. To him the sunrise on the desert was the most beautiful sight in the world. Or the second most beautiful now that he'd seen Melissa.

He felt at ease with himself as he stood looking at the white clouds reflecting the pink and gold of the sun that was just peeping over the mountains.

It's too bad, he thought, that people just can't enjoy all the good things in life instead of trying to get more than their share. Here was this beautiful morning. He was with a gorgeous woman and it could turn into a special day if it weren't for people like the Dayton brothers.

Even the horses seemed happy as they munched contentedly on grass that looked like it had been shot through and through with green. A gentle wind, with the fresh, washed smell of earth in it, whispered across the land.

The sky was a clear blue except for a few scattered white clouds. But from all past experiences, Drew knew that it would be another hot day.

Melissa was still asleep when he went back inside the cabin. She lay on her side, looking as comfortable as if she were in the suite at the Grand Hotel in Philadelphia. Wonder what she's dreaming about, Drew wondered as she smiled in her sleep, a dimple at the corner of her mouth. As he stuck wood in the stove to make a fresh fire, the noise awakened her.

"Good morning," he said cheerfully, smiling down at her as he poured water and coffee in the pot and sat it on the stove.

"I guess so," she replied drowsily, sitting up and pushing her tousled hair back from her face. She gasped in pain as her sore muscles rebelled again when she tried to stand up. But she got to her feet with a little less effort than yesterday morning.

"Need some help?" Drew asked, watching her.

"No, thank you," she answered quickly, squinting her eyes together as she slowly straightened up. "As soon as my bones realize that they haven't died, they'll make it." He laughed when she said that, appreciating her sense of humor in such a situation.

Pouring a little water on a handkerchief, she dabbed it to her face and neck and then wiped her hands.

Drew poured batter into a skillet and put it on the front of the stove. It didn't take long for the thin bread to cook. While he was doing this, Melissa stood watching him.

"I don't suppose there's any chance for a bath," she asked, sitting down at the table. Drew noticed that she hadn't looked directly at him since she had gotten up and he knew that she was embarrassed about his kissing her last night.

"Afraid not," he said, pouring black steaming coffee into a tin cup and handing it to her. Their fingers touched briefly. "Guess what we're having for breakfast this morning?" he asked, smiling down at her bent head.

"Oh, let me see," she said, finally looking up at him and turning pink. Propping her elbows on the table, she dropped her chin on upturned palms. "I think," she said slowly, "that it will be coffee, beans, and bread."

"That's right," Drew beamed at her. "You win and here's your prize," he said, cutting off a wedge of hot bread and spooning beans into her plate.

"Will we reach Tucson today?" Melissa asked, after swallowing a fork full of beans. Drew gazed at her over the rim of his coffee cup. He expected to find an eagerness in her eyes. But instead he saw a wistfulness there.

"If the Daytons don't find us and the sky doesn't unload anymore, we will," he answered, draining his cup.

"The Daytons," she said. It wasn't a question. It was merely a statement. "We haven't seen them since day before yesterday. Do you actually believe they're following us?"

"Miss Dunbar," Drew said, pushing the chair back and standing up, "if I'm never sure of anything else in my life, I'm positive that the Daytons are following us."

She helped him clean the things away. "This time," he said to her smiling broadly, "I'm going to let you wash all of the dishes. Even the coffeepot. We won't be needing them anymore."

She looked around at him and again a sadness filled her eyes. They each picked up their dried clothes from where they'd been spread yesterday and tied them up in the bedrolls.

Melissa's dress was dry and she could have put it on.

"No, I'll keep these clothes on," she said. "As much as I dislike to admit it, the colonel was right. These pants and shirt are more comfortable to ride a horse in."

Drew knew that it took a lot for her to make such a confession. Picking up the saddle bags, bedrolls, and water canteens, Drew went outside to saddle the horses.

With slow and deliberate care, Drew saddled the two horses, telling himself that he wanted it done right. He didn't want to admit to himself that he wanted to stay with Melissa as long as he could. But that was silly.

As soon as she's in Tucson, he told himself, tightening the cinch, you'll forget all about her. And you know that she will certainly forget about you. When she's back with people of her own class, probably Charles Sinclair or someone like him, you will be the last thing on her mind. Shrugging his shoulders, he gave the cinch a savage jerk.

Just as he finished saddling the last horse, he heard a sound like two boards slamming together. At the same instant, he heard Melissa scream.

"Drew, Help!" her voice rang out, wild with panic.

Drew's nerves tensed and he had the gut feeling that their time had just run out. With the other bedroll still in his hand, Drew whirled around. But he wasn't ready for what he saw.

Leaning nonchalantly against the front of the shack was Cap Dayton! His arms were crossed loosely over his thick chest and a sneering smile flattened his thick nose against his face. Drew looked around quickly for the other two brothers. But they were nowhere to be seen.

Then he remembered Melissa's scream. It still echoed in his head. That meant that Tom and Slade were inside the shack with her!

Drew made a slight movement to draw his gun. But Cap drew his Colt .45 with such lightning speed that it banished all thought from Drew's mind of drawing his own gun and he froze where he stood.

"Now that's bein' real smart," Cap complimented, still grinning. Drew had always considered himself to be extra good with a gun. In his line of work, he had to be or he wouldn't last very long. But he had to admit that Cap Dayton was a lot better than he was and he knew that it would be very foolish to try and beat him. Some other way would have to be used to beat Cap.

"Don't try to do nuthin' funny, mister," Cap drawled in his raspy voice, knowing and enjoying the fact that he was in total command at the moment. "Just drop your bedroll like it was hot and raise your hands."

Drew, never having been one who needed to be told twice what to do, complied without hesitation.

"Now, put your right hand behind your head," Cap went on, "and undo that gunbelt with your left hand."

When Drew was disarmed, Cap said, "Now let's walk real easy-like inside." Cap bent down, picked up Drew's gun belt, and followed him inside.

As they went into the shack, Drew saw Slade and Tom sitting at the table, each with a gun leveled at Melissa. She stood at the far side of the table nearest the stove, her face pale and her eyes big. If the situation hadn't been so dangerous, Drew would have laughed. Two grown men holding loaded guns on one defenseless woman. Or was she so defenseless?

"Well, well, I think you folks tried to pull a fast one on us yesterday," Cap said with a rueful smile that bared his yellow teeth. He slammed the door shut behind them and dropped Drew's gun on the floor.

"Yeah, tellin' us that you was married," Tom said with a sneering laugh and slapping his leg.

"We looked real stupid all right," Slade said, pushing his battered hat back on his head. "stoppin' that stage way out in the middle of nowhere and nobody in it. But we really did look stupid when we got to that way station and you and your wife and her brother wasn't even there and neither was Melissa Dunbar."

Drew and Melissa exchanged quick looks. Apparently Charles Sinclair had hidden after they had left him at the way station or he had gotten a stage before the Daytons had arrived there.

"Well, now," Cap drawled, sitting down on the edge of the table, "how could Melissa Dunbar be there when she was with . . . what did you say your name was again?" Cap asked Drew with a shrewdness in his voice.

"His name is Drew Williams and he is my husband," Melissa insisted, terror at the edge of her voice and she started to take a step toward Drew.

"Now hold it, Miss Dunbar," Tom warned softly, pointing his gun at Drew's middle. "Don't try to play us for a bunch of fools. Just because we believed you one time, it don't mean we'll do it again."

"Wait a minute," Slade yelled, jumping

up from the chair and looking around the room. Without saying anything else, he rushed over to the door to the dirt-floored room. Jerking the door open, he looked around inside, then slammed the door shut.

"Slade, what in the devil do you think you're doin'?" Cap asked slowly, throwing a frowning look at his brother.

"That other guy, her brother," Slade said, pointing to Melissa, a bewildered look on his bearded face. "He's gone. Why ain't he here?"

Cap spun around facing Drew. "Where is he? Where's he hidin'?"

There was no danger to Charles Sinclair now, so Drew didn't see anything wrong in telling them that they had been made a fool of another time.

"If he didn't catch a stage while you were waiting for the one you thought Melissa Dunbar was riding, " Drew said with raised eyebrows, "he was right there under your nose at the way station."

"That's two mistakes we made yesterday," Tom said furiously, kicking the chair out of his way.

"No," Drew said calmly. "You made three mistakes yesterday."

"What was the third?" Tom asked frowning, leveling a cold look at Drew.

"Getting up," Drew replied.

"Okay," Cap interrupted, "cut the funny stuff. It'll be easy enough to find out if you're Clara Williams or Melissa Dunbar. Who gave you that ring?" Cap asked, pointing to the pearl ring that she wore on her right hand.

"Why?" Melissa asked, clutching her right hand fearfully to her chest.

"Who give you that ring?" Cap demanded in a shout, slamming his fist down against the table, his green eyes flashing in a rage. "I ain't playin' games with you, lady!"

"My father did," she replied softly. "But that wouldn't prove if I'm Clara Williams or Melissa Dunbar." She tried to sound brave. But inside she was scared to death, having no idea what the man had in mind.

"Well, Senator Dunbar would know it if he saw it, wouldn't he?" Cap asked, a sly grin on his mouth. "That is, if you are Melissa Dunbar and I think you are."

Cap got up from the table and came toward her. She started to take a step toward Drew. But Cap reached out and grabbed her hand. In one swift motion, he pulled the ring from her finger. Jerking her hand from his, Melissa wiped it on the seat of her britches, a nauseating look on her face at being touched by such a filthy man. Dayton only laughed at her action.

"So you don't like bein' touched by me, huh, little lady?" Cap asked, reaching out his hand to touch her face.

Drew didn't stop to think about the consequences of his action. He just grabbed Melissa by the arm and swung her around behind him. He could feel the warmth of her trembling hand on his back.

"Don't press your luck, Dayton," Drew said, glaring at him with a threatening note in his voice.

"Williams, I could drop you right where you stand," Tom said, cocking the hammer back on the pistol.

"Now, Tom," Cap said slowly, dropping his hand, "he's just showin' off for Miss Dunbar. Let's don't rush things. We're in a good place to keep Miss Dunbar company."

Cap looked around the cabin and nodded his head in satisfaction. "We couldn't have found a better place if we'd been lookin' for one." He smiled, very pleased with himself.

"Keep her company?" Drew repeated, looking quickly back at Melissa and then at Cap. "What do you mean? If you hurt her, you'll have the army after you. Not to mention me."

"Now you'll be an easy matter to take care of," Slade said, cocking the hammer back on his pistol.

"If the army couldn't send an armed guard with her," Tom asked, "why would they be so hot to come after us?"

These men sure are in a hurry to kill me, Drew told himself, watching them play with their guns.

"Not now, Slade, Tom," Cap said in an easy voice, "there's time."

"We're not goin' to hurt her, Williams," Tom said, with an ugly laugh. "We're just goin' to see how anxious Senator Dunbar is to sign a paper with a bunch of savages. I imagine when Cap gets back, you both can go."

"What makes you think that?" Drew asked, watching him suspiciously.

"Because," Cap answered, "when the senator

sees that we mean business and have found his daughter, he'll know that if he does sign that agreement, we'll kill her. If he don't sign it, we won't. It's that simple."

That didn't even make sense to Drew. But he wasn't about to argue the point and make him mad.

Cap walked to the door, putting the ring in his pocket. "Since we rode all night in the rain, Williams, and your horses are rested, I'll just borrow one of them."

"Want us to tie them up?" Tom asked, standing up, his gun aimed at Drew.

"No," Cap answered irritably. "Can't the two of you handle them? You've got guns. Just keep your eyes open. Williams don't wear a gun tied down for nuthin'."

Dayton jerked the door open and slammed it shut behind him. A few seconds later they heard the sounds of disappearing horse's hooves. The remaining four people stood looking at each other for a moment.

"Well," Tom said, dragging a chair over by the door. He sat down and tipped it back against the wall. "I guess we might as well get comfortable until Cap comes back."

For a while all was quiet in the cabin except for the popping of the stove cooling. Melissa and Drew exchanged quick glances, each knowing that time was wasting. Drew knew that they were safe until Cap returned. But he didn't want to wait that long.

"May I put that bench in the corner and sit down?" Melissa asked Tom in a trembling voice. "I don't feel well." Drew wasn't used to women's ways and couldn't tell if she was acting or not.

"Sure, ma'am," Tom replied, lazily running his gaze boldly up and down her figure, letting his eyes rest on the pockets of the shirt and the rounded hips.

Drew didn't think she was going to faint. If she didn't faint when she saw that snake yesterday, she wasn't about to faint now. Looking at Drew with a burning intensity, Melissa flashed her eyes to the bench and back to him.

"I'll take it for you," Drew said, catching on as he picked up the bench and followed her to the opposite side of the room. Turning abruptly, he put himself between her and the two outlaws, his back to them. With quick fingers, she reached inside her shirt and withdrew a small two-shot derringer and thrust it into his shirt. He didn't move his hands to avoid suspicion from the other men. Then she quickly sat down on the crude bench.

"Miss Dunbar isn't feeling well," Drew said, turning around and facing the Daytons, dropping the pretense of being married to her. His mind was racing. She was trying to give him some kind of chance. "She needs a drink of water and the canteens are on the horses."

Drew knew that they wouldn't let him go outside. But he started walking toward the door anyway. At least he'd be close to one of them when the other went outside for the water.

"Hold on there," Tom snapped, jumping up from his chair by the door and drawing his gun. "Where do you think you're goin'?"

"For water," Drew replied simply. "Miss Dunbar needs a drink."

"I'll get the water," Slade said, getting up from his chair at the table and swaggering toward the door. "Watch 'em, Tom," he commanded over his shoulder.

There wasn't very much time. Drew knew that he'd have to work fast. He glanced over his shoulder at Melissa. Her head was back against the wall and her eyes were closed. Her arms lay limply at her sides. But Drew noticed that she was breathing as regularly as the situation would let anyone breathe.

"She's fainted," Drew said, hurrying back to her, genuine concern in his voice. "Let's lay her on the floor."

Tom walked slowly toward them, holstering his gun. Drew quickly reached into his shirt, withdrawing the derringer. The small gun was completely hidden in Drew's hand and like a cat, with one swing of his paw, Drew hit Tom an unconscious-rendering blow on the left side of his jaw. Knowing that he wouldn't have time for a second chance, Drew had put all of his strength into the lick. Dayton hit the floor without making a sound, never knowing what had happened to him.

Melissa's eyes flew open when she heard the man hit the floor and she jumped up from the bench.

"Is he dead?" she asked, looking down at the still form on the floor. Her eyes were wide and fearful. Apparently she'd never seen a dead man.

"No," Drew answered, quickly jerking Tom's gun from the holster and handed Melissa her little gun. Drew pulled Tom's limp body over by the wall where it would be out of sight and dropped him just in time to get over to the door as Slade opened it, carrying a canteen in each hand.

Thank the Lord these men aren't too bright, Drew prayed silently.

When Slade didn't see Tom sitting by the door where he'd left him, he knew instantly that they'd been tricked again and dropped the canteens. The jolt jarred the cap from one and water ran freely across the floor. Dayton made a feeble effort to go for his gun.

But he wasn't quite as fast as Cap. Drew caught him across the jaw with the barrel of Tom's gun. With a painful grunt, Slade went down unconscious. Drew quickly picked up his own gun belt, strapped it around his lean waist, and tied it to his leg.

"Why didn't you shoot him?" Melissa asked, looking at the other unconscious man.

"There was no need to," Drew replied, checking the shells in the pistol.

"Are you going after the other man?" she asked, glancing from one unconscious man on the floor to the other. The little gun that she'd given to Drew was nowhere in sight.

"Yes," Drew replied, glancing over at Tom by the wall. He was beginning to come around. "As soon as I tie these two up," he said. "Cap shouldn't be too far ahead. I hate to tell you this. But you're going to have to stay here and guard them."

"What?" she asked horrified, spinning around to face him, her brown eyes boring into his. "You can't be serious! Why can't we take them with us and go on to Tucson?" She stared at him, her eyes big and frightened. "They might get untied and kill me!"

"Dayton would have a better chance of jumping you and me with his brothers along than just me," Drew said. "It's better if I go alone. I can make better time this way. But I'll make guarding them easy," Drew told her with a wink and a grin.

"Whatever you say," Melissa replied in a weary voice. She didn't know what he had in mind until he went outside and came back with his saddle bags. There was a gleam in his eyes.

"I'm glad that Dayton took your horse instead of mine," Drew said, reaching into the bag and bringing out four long, thin rawhide strings. Each string was about a foot long and about as thick as two shoestrings together.

"What are those?" Melissa asked, watching him straighten them out.

"Rawhide strips that I use for boot lacings," he told her.

Tom was completely conscious now but he was too groggy to do anything. Drew turned him over on his stomach, tied his hands behind his back and pulled him to his feet.

"You won't get away with this, Williams," Tom muttered thickly. "When Cap catches you, he'll blow your head off and I have a pretty good idea what he'll do to her," nodding toward Melissa.

"You'd better worry about what he'll do to you," Drew told him, "for getting into this." Drew marched him outside. He was gone for a few minutes, then came back inside and tied the still unconscious Slade's hands behind his back and dragged him outside.

Melissa, completely speechless and having no idea at all what Drew was going to have her do, followed him. There were a few small trees on the north side of the cabin that they hadn't seen in the rain yesterday. Tom was sitting in the scant shade of the smallest tree and Drew dragged Slade over by him.

"You won't get away with this," Tom growled in a voice full of hatred. "When Cap hears about this, he'll kill you." There was a stony look in Tom's eyes and Drew knew that if Tom could get loose right now, he'd save Cap the trouble.

"Not if I see him first, he won't," Drew promised coldly, testing the knots.

"Are you going to leave them there like that?" Melissa asked, looking down at the two bound men speculatively.

Drew didn't wait to ask her if she meant no more guarded than they were or being tied and out in the sparse shade.

"No," he answered quickly, realizing that time was slipping away. Running over to the Daytons' horses, Drew cut off one of the reins and came back to where the men were sitting. Drew tied the already bound hands together and then to the trunk of the tree. Getting a canteen he poured water on the rawhide strips.

"Now, if you boys won't try to get loose, the strips won't dry too fast and cut your hands. You know what dry rawhide will do," Drew said. Having taken both men's guns, he handed one to Melissa and shoved the other one in his waistband.

"If one does try to get loose," he instructed, "shoot them both in the leg. Don't get close to them and don't fall for any of their tricks."

"When will you be back?" Melissa asked, as she stood holding the big pistol in her hands.

"Just as soon as I find Dayton," Drew replied softly, wishing he didn't have to leave her in this situation.

"Are you going to kill him?" she asked, looking up at him, anxiety in her eyes.

"Not unless I have to," Drew answered. He waited until she sat down in the shade of the largest tree, a little distance from the Daytons. Then he quickly bent down, turned her face up with a finger under her chin, and kissed her parted lips.

Without a backward look, he mounted his horse in a running jump, kicked the animal in the side, and headed north in the direction that Cap Dayton had taken not more than twenty minutes ago.

Making good time on the rested animal, Drew followed the hoof marks that a child could have tracked. Dayton wasn't making any effort to hide his trail, but then, why should he? Drew and the horse made good time. He let the animal run as hard as he wanted to. The morning was cool and the horse wasn't tiring out.

Drew rode out of a gulch and topped a hill with a view of the valley below. Drew jerked the horse to a startled stop. For a moment he couldn't believe what he saw.

Down below, a group of Indians formed a semicircle facing a rock. From where he was, Drew counted eight men.

Three Indians were kneeling on the ground beside a still figure. The rest of the Indians remained mounted. From the distance Drew couldn't tell why the man was on the ground or who he was.

One of the mounted men on a solid black stallion wore the full dress of a chief. The white feathered headdress, with red and blue tips, hung down his back. His buckskin britches and shirt were also white. A rifle lay across his knees.

Hearing the horse approach, all of the Indians turned in Drew's direction. Coming closer to them, Drew recognized Chief Half Moon, having met the chief at Fort Rather last year, and raised his hand in greeting. The chief smiled at Drew, if a minute twitch of the bronze face could be called a smile and he raised his hand in similar greeting.

Drew was close enough now for a full view of the still figure on the ground. A board across the face or a kick in the stomach by a mule couldn't have taken him more by surprise.

It was Cap Dayton!

He was leaning back against the boulder and it would have been easy to believe that he was just sitting there resting, his arms limply at his side. Easy, that is, if it hadn't been for the arrow embedded deeply into the center of his dirty green shirt. A red blotch had spread across his chest and a trickle of blood ran from the corner of his mouth and mingled with the dust in his beard. The washed-out and sightless eyes stared at nothing.

Cap Dayton was dead!

Why would Half Moon let one of his braves kill the man who had been giving them guns for so long? Something was wrong here.

"What happened?" Drew asked Half Moon as he dismounted and knelt beside the lifeless body of Cap Dayton.

"He saw us coming from ridge," Half Moon explained, pointing to the hill from where Drew had just come. The Indian continued in jerking English. "Before we could talk, he shot Swift Elk. Then Little Bear put arrow in him. He was a bad man. Is that not so?" There was no emotion in the black eyes and his face was immobile.

"Yes," Drew agreed, "he was a bad man. But why would he want to shoot one of your men? You and he have been doing business together for a long time." It was a known fact that Dayton and Half Moon had dealt in guns, but Drew wasn't sure how the Indian would take the accusation.

"Maybe we surprise him," Half Moon suggested. "Maybe he thought he would scare us and we would not sign paper with Senator Dunbar."

Drew pondered this for a moment. That could be a reason. Dayton could have thought that if one of Half Moon's men was killed by him, Half Moon wouldn't be so eager to sign a paper and take a chance of getting more of his men killed.

"Where was he going?" Half Moon asked, watching Drew. He wasn't sure what the frown on Drew's tanned face meant.

"He was on his way to Tucson with the ring of Senator Dunbar's daughter," Drew said. "His two brothers are being guarded by her now."

"One woman guards Tom and Slade Dayton?" Half Moon asked with slightly raised eyebrows, a note of disbelief in his voice. For the first time, an expression crossed the Indian's face. A puzzled and bewildered look twinkled in his black eyes.

"I would like to see this," he said, nodding his head slightly. The brightly colored feathers shook a little.

"Where are you heading?" Drew asked, knowing that the signing wasn't to take place for a few more days yet.

"To Fort Rather," Half Moon said. "The paper is to be signed days from now. We thought we go early and talk to Colonel Walters until Senator Dunbar comes."

When Half Moon mentioned Dunbar, Drew remembered Melissa's ring. He walked over to the still body on the ground, bent down, and took the ring from the bloody pocket. Pouring water from a canteen over it, Drew dried it with his bandanna. He looked at it for a moment, then put it in his shirt pocket, and buttoned the flap.

Then Drew and one of the Indians picked

up Cap's limp body, laid it across the saddle, and tied it with a rope. Drew removed the saddle bags and bedroll from the horse and tied it with his own.

"Where are you going?" Half Moon asked.

"I was taking Miss Dunbar to her father in Tucson," Drew explained. "His birthday is today and she wanted to give him a party tonight. Now I've got more on my hands than I had counted on."

"What do you mean?" Half Moon asked, gazing steadily at Drew.

"Well," Drew answered, pushing his hat back on his head, "if I take Miss Dunbar and the Daytons back to the fort, we'll lose two days and she'll miss her father's party. I couldn't take her back there with a dead man along anyway. I can't take the Daytons to Tucson for the same reason."

Drew threw his hands up in the air in a helpless gesture and with a disdainful expression on his face.

"Since we go to fort," Half Moon said, "we take Daytons for you. We can also see woman guarding other Dayton men."

Drew wasn't too crazy about Half Moon's idea. He knew that the Daytons wouldn't like it any better than he did. But he really didn't have any choice. By the time they went back to Fort Rather to take the Daytons, they would lose three days. But it wouldn't be fair to Melissa to take the Daytons to Tucson with one of them being dead.

So Drew had to rely on the Indians.

Before they mounted, Drew looked around

for the body of the dead Indian. "Where's Swift Elk's body?" Drew asked.

"Little Fox take him back to village," Half Moon said.

When they were all mounted and the lifeless body tied securely, they started out on the short ride back to the cabin. The only sound was that of the unshod Indian horses' hooves on the ground and the creaking of Drew's saddle and the other one over which Cap Dayton's body was tied.

Soon the ride was over and the cabin came into view. Melissa was still sitting in the shade of the tree, her legs stretched out in front of her and crossed at the ankles. The big pistol lay in her lap.

Melissa, seeing the Indians, scrambled up, dropping the gun. She clasped her hands to her face and screamed. She hadn't expected them and she hadn't seen Drew who rode on the opposite side of Half Moon. Everything she'd ever heard about savage Indians popped into her mind. She could see herself being scalped and clubbed to death with a tomahawk.

Drew quickly dismounted and hurried over to her. "It's all right," he said, putting his arm around her shoulders. "That's Chief Half Moon. Did you have any trouble out of them?" he asked, nodding toward the men under the other tree.

"No," she answered, looking up at him. "I guess they were afraid that if they did try to scare me, I would shoot them." A smile brightened her face and Drew grinned down at her.

"If a woman had a gun aimed at me," he

said, "I wouldn't try anything." He laughed at the quizzical look she gave him. I'm glad that she didn't have a gun last night, he told himself, thinking about kissing her. But then he remembered that she'd had that little gun. "Come over here and meet the chief," he said, taking her arm.

"Why did she scream?" Half Moon asked, still mounted, as they approached.

Melissa dropped her head in embarrassment at having acted so foolish.

"Chief," Drew said, still holding her by the arm as they stood by the black horse, "this is Melissa Dunbar, the daughter of Senator Dunbar. She's from the eastern part of the country and isn't used to some of our ways." Turning, he went back to the tied Daytons under the tree.

"Chief, I'm so glad to meet you," Melissa said, smiling up at him not certain if she should offer her hand or bow to him, so she did neither.

"I hope paper I sign with your father will be a good one," Half Moon said with a slight nod.

The horse carrying Cap Dayton's body had been at the end of the group. The two brothers didn't see it until Drew cut the reins from the tree and they got stiffly to their feet. Slade saw the body first, then Tom saw it.

"Who's tied on that horse?" Slade asked, looking at the horse and its burden.

"It's Cap, ain't it?" Tom asked before Drew could answer, the color draining from his face.

The two brothers broke into a run toward the horse. Neither Drew nor the Indians tried to stop them. With their hands tied and so many armed men around, they couldn't go very far or do anything anyway.

"Who killed him?" Slade demanded, spinning around to face Drew, a look of green hatred in his black eyes.

"You probably waited for him in an ambush," Tom accused in a roar. "With Cap dead, you thought you wouldn't have to sign that paper with Dunbar. But you've took guns from us and you raided coaches and settlements. You're in this as deep as we are."

"We not ambush," Half Moon said simply, shaking his head defiantly. "He shot Swift Elk first. Only reason we took guns from you was to get food from you after you kill so many buffalo. Army has promised they will help us if we sign paper. It is time we go. Get on your horses."

"What does he mean?" Slade asked, giving Drew a sideways glance, his eyes narrowing.

"Half Moon and his men are going to take you and Tom back to Fort Rather," Drew answered, looking Dayton straight in the eye.

"You've got to be crazy, Williams!" Tom screamed, his eyes wide in fear. "He'll kill us the first chance he gets."

"Not if you behave yourselves, he won't," Drew said, walking toward the Indians, a perplexed expression in his eyes. "Chief, I want your word that no harm will come to these men. I want them to be in one piece when I get back to the fort."

"It is yours," Half Moon said solemnly. He reached down and shook Drew's hand. A gesture that he didn't do very often. The two Daytons struggled but got on their horses by themselves. As they moved away, Slade stopped his horse directly in front of Drew.

"You're to blame for this, Williams," he accused through clenched teeth, his eyes blazing. "I'll get you for it if it's the last thing I do."

Drew knew that it was no idle threat that Slade made. Men such as the Daytons didn't say things that they didn't mean. Drew was very positive that he'd meet Slade and Tom Dayton again over guns.

"Do you think he means it, Drew?" Melissa asked, calling him by his first name as he helped her up on the horse. He was a little surprised and greatly pleased that she had called him by his first name.

"Oh, he means it, all right," Drew answered, glancing over his shoulder at the disappearing cloud of dust. "I don't doubt that sometime in the very near future, Slade Dayton will make good the promise he just made."

"Aren't you afraid?" she asked, staring at him.

"No," he replied simply. "I've been threatened before. I take each day as it comes and hope that the good Lord is watching over me."

"By the way," she said, still watching him, "did you get my ring?"

"Yes," he replied, taking the ring from his pocket and handing it to her. He didn't tell her about the blood that had been on it.

The sun was well up in the sky when they finally left the cabin.

"How long will it be before we reach Tucson?" Melissa asked, riding beside him. Even though she wore pants, she still rode with her right leg around the saddle horn.

"We should be there about four o'clock," Drew answered, turning his head to face her. "I guess you'll be glad for all of this to end."

"I'm very anxious to see my father," she answered, smiling slightly. "I haven't seen him in three months. But it's really a trip that I will never forget."

Drew liked hearing her soft voice as she talked. After she'd come down from her high horse, she was much nicer to be with. Drew knew that after he left her in Tucson, he would think about her for a long, long time.

But hope sprang up in him when she said that she'd never forget this trip.

"Why do you say this is something you'll never forget?" he asked, wanting her to keep on talking. "Surely, you've been on much more exciting trips than this?"

"Well, in all of my wildest dreams," she said, shaking her head, "I never expected to be riding a horse and wearing someone else's clothes," she went on with a laugh. "I never expected to see Indians and hold a gun on two men who wanted to kidnap me all in the same day. If someone had told me two months ago or even last week, that I, a senator's daughter, would spend a night sleeping on the ground and another in an old shack with a man I didn't know, I would have told them they were out of their mind." A becoming blush colored her face and she dropped her gaze from his.

"Don't forget Charles Sinclair and that snake back there at the river," Drew reminded her.

"Oh, I was going to save that for last," she said, smiling broadly enough to bring out the dimples at the corner of her mouth. "I think I was more frightened of that snake even after you said that it wasn't poison than I was of the Dayton men."

"Why?" Drew asked, frowning at her, not following her logic.

"Well, I know that if a poison snake bites you and you don't get help quickly, you'll die," she explained. "In the Daytons' case, I was too valuable to kill."

"What about Charles Sinclair?" Drew asked.

"Charles Sinclair should have stayed in Philadelphia or in England," she said, looking back at him and shrugging her shoulders. "There he wouldn't have looked so ridiculous in those clothes."

Drew threw back his head and laughed uproariously. Then he sobered when he remembered that she hadn't mentioned the kisses.

"Is that all you're going to remember?" he asked, holding her gaze in a long look. His heart turned over in his chest when a soft expression came into her eyes. They were just like the fawn's. Soft and deep and warm. She turned a deeper pink, knowing what he was talking about.

Before lowering her eyes from his again, she shook her head. "No, that isn't all that I'm going to remember."

Chapter Five

Noon found Drew and Melissa at a clear-water pool and they took a rest stop. Sitting on the edge of the bank, they nibbled on cold bread and beans from breakfast.

"Would you like to take a bath and change your clothes?" Drew asked.

"Take a bath?" she repeated, her eyes wide, looking around with trepidation. "Where?"

"Right there in the pool," Drew said, pointing to the water.

"Oh, no," Melissa refused, shaking her head quickly, giving him an impish sideways look. "As soon as I'd get in the water something would happen to my clothes."

"You don't think I'd hide your clothes, do you?" Drew asked, a mock indignation in his eyes, along with a gleam.

"Yes, I do," she answered simply. "Besides, I've become accustomed to these old clothes and hat."

She'd stuffed her long hair up under the hat and turned the shirt collar up around her neck. Without the parasol to shade her neck, it was turning pink.

"Haven't you ever seen a woman ride astride before?" she asked as she swung her right leg over the saddle when Drew helped her mount, amused at his astonishment.

"Sure," he replied. "But not you. Why have you waited until the end of the trip to ride more comfortably?"

"Well, I just wanted to see if you and the colonel really knew what you were talking about," she answered, nodding her head.

Drew looked over at her hands holding the reins in a loose grip. They were red now from the sun whereas they'd been milk white just three days ago.

Three days ago! It seemed impossible that he'd met her just three days ago. He was really sorry that the trip was almost over. Drew knew that she would be coming back to the fort with her father in a couple of days. But the colonel would probably have another job for him away from the fort.

He got the sinking feeling in the middle of his stomach thinking that he might never see her again.

Almost as if she'd read his thoughts, she asked, "Will you be at Fort Rather when I get . . . I mean . . . when we get back?"

"Probably not," he answered, shaking his head. "I never know from one day to the next where I'll be. There are a lot of wagon trains coming through now and the people usually want a guide through what they call 'hostile country.' "

"Does this job pay sufficiently?" she asked. Then she wished that she hadn't asked such a personal question. She realized that she probably spent more on clothes on one buying trip than he earned in a month.

"Well, it keeps a shirt on my back," he replied with a shrug and smile, "and food in my stomach. One good thing about it is that you get to go a lot of places and meet a lot of different people."

"Have you ever had to be in charge of just one person before?" she asked.

"No," he replied, looking ahead and seeing the silhouette of Tucson. "It's usually a wagon train or at least a small group of people."

It was about four thirty when they arrived in Tucson. Only half an hour later than Drew had predicted.

"My father will really be surprised to see me dressed like this," she said, changing the subject and looking down at the shirt and pants. "After Mother died, I stayed in boarding schools in Philadelphia. He's always wanted me to dress and act the part of the spoiled rich girl. So he will probably have a fit and faint." She laughed and it sounded like bells again.

Drew hadn't forgotten the haughtiness she'd displayed the other day in Colonel Walters' office. He preferred this girl to that one.

"He'll probably faint," she continued, smiling at him mischievously, "when he finds out that I slept on the ground, got soaking wet, and had to guard two outlaws."

"That'll really be a tale to tell your grandchildren," Drew teased, smiling back at her, "when you're old and gray."

"Grandchildren?" she gasped. "I'll have to

find a husband first," she replied, giving him a beguiling smile.

"That shouldn't be too hard for a girl with your looks," he said. "There's always Charles Sinclair, you know." Drew still wanted to know what she really thought about Sinclair and had intended to find out before they reached Tucson.

"Charles Sinclair?" she asked blankly. Then she rolled her eyes skyward as reality struck. "You're joking! After he deserted us in the middle of nowhere? I know he wasn't any help to you. But he could have at least come along and tried to be more of the man he'd bragged about being on the trip out here from Philadelphia. Charles Sinclair? No thanks. I told you before that he should have stayed back East. How about your own grandchildren?"

Her question caught him off guard and he had to think for a minute. "There aren't many women who'd want to marry an army scout," he finally answered, puzzled at her question. "Their future is too uncertain. Would you?" he asked, a mock and challenging gleam in his eyes.

With raised eyebrows, she pursed her lips. "It would depend entirely on the army scout. No one's future is really certain, for that matter."

By now they'd reached the hotel. Drew tied the horses and for the last time that he knew, helped Melissa dismount, standing her down on the ground with his hands still around her small waist. He looked deep into her eyes and probably would have kissed her if he hadn't heard an urgent voice.

"Melissa? Is that you?"

Drew guessed that the tall silver-haired man rushing in long strides down the steps toward them was Senator Dunbar. He must have been waiting for them and seen them coming because he was out of the hotel so quickly. Drew saw a stricken expression cross the man's tanned face as he looked at Melissa. He really looked like he'd faint.

Before the man put his arm around Melissa's shoulders, he asked, almost demanding, "Melissa, why in the world are you wearing those old clothes? Who do they belong to? Where did you get them? Where are your own things?"

"Hello, Papa, it's good to see you, too," Melissa said, smiling up at him. "See what I told you," she said over her shoulder to Drew. "Papa, this is Drew Williams. He's the one who brought me through peril and pain."

"Pain?" the senator repeated, stepping back and looking her up and down, a worried expression in his blue eyes. "What pain? What happened? Are you all right?"

The questions came so rapidly that Melissa didn't have time to answer the first one. She was touched by his concern and knew that he'd had a long and nervous wait. He gripped her shoulders and stared down at her.

"I'll tell you all about it later, Papa," she said, patting him on the arm and smiling up at him. Her brown eyes danced as she kissed him on the cheek. "Right now all I want is a long, hot bath."

Drew came up by her on the porch, handing her one of the bedrolls. She took it and smiled up at him. He started down the steps when he heard her call him. "Drew, you will be at the party tonight, won't you?" she asked, coming back down the steps to stand by him. She looked up at him with warm brown eyes and rested her hand on his arm as she waited for his answer. Her touch was warm and burned through the sleeve of his shirt.

"I will if you want me to," Drew replied, placing his hand over hers. He hadn't expected to go to the party and was surprised that she invited him.

"After all that we've been through together?" she asked with twinkling eyes and raised eyebrows. "Of course, I want you to be there. Come about seven thirty."

With a nod, he untied the horses and led them down the street to the livery stable. While he unsaddled them and took off the other bedroll, he realized that he didn't have anything nice enough to wear to the senator's birthday party.

Never a vain man, Drew's appearance hadn't been a bother to him as long as his clothes were clean. But he'd never gone to a senator's party before. He knew that it wouldn't do to show up dressed the way he was.

"Where's a good place to buy clothes?" Drew asked the livery man.

"Oppenheimer's is a good place," was the reply. "It's across the street and two doors up."

The store was really a clothing store, one of the few that Drew had been in. Women's clothes on one side and men's and children's on the other. Drew had never seen such a selection before. But then he'd never had the need before.

A little man with bald head and round belly came shuffling toward him. "Need some help, sir?" he asked eagerly, peering at Drew through little gold round-rimmed glasses, taking in every detail of Drew's clothes.

He started at the top of Drew's full head of long brown hair and, like Colonel Walters, envied him.

Then he ticked off the faded blue shirt and black pants and wished that he could wear moccasin boots instead of the sensible shoes he had to wear because of fallen arches.

"Yes, I need a suit for a party tonight," Drew answered, suddenly embarrassed that he was buying a suit to please a girl. He knew he wouldn't have gone even if the senator himself had invited him. But he knew that Melissa would be dressed in her finest and he wanted her to be glad to see him again.

He could almost picture her in the blue dress that he'd folded for her to put in the saddle bag. He wasn't much on describing dresses, but he knew that it had long lace sleeves and the neck wasn't very high.

"Guess you're going to the senator's party, huh?" the little man asked, "Would you want something elegant or plain?"

"Oh, a little of both, I guess," Drew answered with a self-conscious grin. "If I'm going to spend money on clothes, I want it to be worthwhile."

"Let's try something in blue first," the little man said. "Most men want black or brown.

But for something special, like a wedding or a party, blue is nice."

He led Drew to the clothes rack, took a dark blue broadcloth coat from a hanger, and held it up in the back for Drew to put on. He had to stand on tiptoe to reach up and smooth the coat across Drew's broad shoulders. But the effort was in vain. It was a size too small across the back and wouldn't button in the front at all.

"You're bigger than I thought," the little man said enviously. "One more came in today," he said, replacing the coat on the hanger. "I'll get it while you try on the pants." In the small dressing room, Drew found that the pants were a better fit than the coat. A tap at the door and the little man handed him the coat. This one fit his broad shoulders as though it had been made just for him.

"Now, I'll need a shirt and tie," Drew said, coming out of the dressing room really pleased with the way he looked. The last two items caused no problem. The white shirt fit nicely and the dark blue string tie added a simple touch of elegance.

With the bundles under his arm, Drew headed for the barber shop. After a haircut and shave, he went back to the hotel and was told that a room was waiting for him when he asked to register. He offered to pay but that had been taken care of, too.

"Senator Dunbar told me not to take your money no matter how much you insisted," the clerk said, tongue in cheek.

Drew nodded, smiled, and looked around

the lobby.

The Burlington Hotel was the finest that Tucson had to offer. In fact, it was the only hotel that Tucson had to offer. But it was an eminent establishment.

Red velvet curtains hung at the wide windows in the lobby of the three story building. Cut glass ashtrays rested on bronze stands beside red velvet chairs. Oriental rugs from San Francisco covered the floor. The mahogany desk, with its marble top, held a leather-bound register book. A gold feathered pen, ink pot, and a silver bell were the only ornaments on the desk.

Most of the keys were gone from the pigeon holes, indicating that the hotel was a popular place to stay.

To the right of the lobby was a dining room that would seat a hundred people and when the tables and chairs were removed, it was an excellent ballroom. There was no bar in the hotel. Woody Burlington thought that a hotel should be apart from a saloon. Only when parties were arranged would he let liquor, and only the best of that, and champagne, be served.

Melissa Dunbar had written Woody Burlington about a month ago and had him make preparations for her father's party tonight. Arranging a party for the senator of the territory would really be a feather in his social cap. He had assured her that everything would be taken care of to her satisfaction.

In his room, Drew looked around at the elaborate furnishings. A brass double bed with a blue satin cover took up most of the room. Duplicates of the lobby curtains hung over the windows. There was a maple washstand with a marble top and splash board. A blue and white procelain water pitcher and washbowl were on it. A dazzling white towel hung on a brass rod beside the washstand.

Two chairs, one like those downstairs and the other a straight-backed wooden one, made up the rest of the furnishings except for the wardrobe with a mirror inside one of the doors. The walls were covered with gold paper and a red and gold rug covered the whole floor.

Drew bathed, washing off the three days accumulation of dust and dirt, and splashed on some of the pine-smelling lotion from a small bottle that he'd bought at the barber shop. When he was finally dressed and stood before the long mirror, he was completely amazed at the difference that the small row of white ruffles on the wrist of the shirt made. His shoulders seemed even broader and his face and hands more brown against the white shirt.

For a moment he thought about wearing a different shirt. This was just too much, he told himself, shaking his head. He was used to wearing open-necked shirts and a bandanna. The buttoned collar and string tie felt like a noose around his neck.

"No," he said, arguing out loud, "she probably thinks that all army scouts are a bunch of rogues and don't know a thing about clothes. Well, she's in for a surprise tonight."

Then he looked down at his moccasins.

Well, you can't give up everything, he chuckled as he left the room and went downstairs.

Melissa had asked him to come at seven thirty and the tall clock in the corner of the lobby chimed the half hour as he opened the dining room door and went in.

The room had undergone as much a transformation as Drew.

Red and white streamers from the center of the ceiling were tacked to the corners of the room. Red, white, and blue balloons hung from the streamers and a huge sign with HAPPY BIRTHDAY, SENATOR DUNBAR covered the entire back wall just over a platform, where a band was to play.

All of the tables except four had been removed. These tables had been put together in a straight line and covered with a white lace cloth over one of red satin. White china plates edged in gold were stacked beside gleaming silver. Little sandwiches, ham cut in bite sizes, and all kinds of relishes took up one end of the table. On the other end of the table was a beautiful white three-tiered cake, with red sugar roses on it, and a bowl of punch, along with several bottles of champagne.

"Do you like it?" asked a soft bell-sounding voice behind him that sent shivers up and down his back. Turning around, he felt his breath catch in his throat. He didn't know whether Melissa was talking about the decorated room or herself. But if she meant herself, he really liked what he saw. He had no idea how she'd accomplished so much in such a short time. But the result was worth the effort.

Her honey-colored hair was pulled up and away from her face with braids and curls. But the dress she wore wasn't the blue one he'd seen before. This one was pale green with just enough color in it to be green at all. The neck bared her slender throat and a little of her shoulders. She wore no jewelry.

The skirt flared out from her small waist and just missed the floor. Long lace sleeves fitted her arms snugly and the color gave a creamy hue to her skin. Her nose was a bit sunburned.

As he stood looking down at her, he noticed the rapid beat of pulse in the hollow of her throat. She's probably been rushing around, he thought. That's why she's so flushed. I guess she changed her mind about wearing the blue dress and bought another one, he reasoned.

"Yes, I like it," he said, smiling down at her and then looking around the room, giving no indication if he meant her or the room. He did notice, however, that she looked pleased and surprised as she gazed up at him with a twinkle in her brown eyes as she took in the way he was dressed.

Before further conversation went on, Melissa glanced over Drew's shoulder at someone approaching, a fond smile replacing the beguiling one she'd used on Drew. "Here comes Papa," she said.

"Mr. Williams," Senator Dunbar said, coming up by them, "I didn't get a chance to thank you properly earlier today. I was just so surprised at the unusual way my daughter was dressed that my manners escaped me." He extended his right hand and grasped Drew's in a firm grip.

"I've known George Walters for many years and I knew that he'd put my daughter under the best protection possible," the senator said, putting his arm around Melissa. "From what she told me there was little to worry about. I must say, though, that I am very disappointed in Charles Sinclair. It's a good thing that I wasn't there when he deserted you. He was always bragging about what a good rider and soldier he was in England. That aristocratic club he belonged to seemed to be always in his mind." The senator's eyes snapped. Drew glanced down at his hands and they were balled up in a tight fist.

"Well, sir," Drew said, "you've got to admit that this country does separate the heroes from the cowards."

"Now, you're not being fair to Charles," Melissa said defensively. "You would probably have done the same thing. He just wasn't used to being threatened with Indians, snakes, and commissioners all in the same day."

Drew and Dunbar exchanged puzzled looks. They stared at each other for a moment. Then Drew burst out laughing. He couldn't have contained himself if his life had depended on it.

"What's so funny?" Melissa asked reproachfully, flashing her eyes from Drew to her father.

"How do you connect commissioners, Indians, and Charles Sinclair?" her father asked, a frown creasing his lean features.

"Well, isn't that what you called the Dayton men?" she asked Drew, her mouth forming a pout.

"Oh, she means commancheros," Drew said, a broad smile spreading across his tanned face.

"Well, anyway," Melissa said, shrugging her shoulders slightly and turning an embarrassed pink. "Besides, he isn't here to defend his actions."

"Well, I'm just glad that you're here," Dunbar said, smiling down at his daughter and then at Drew. "There are some things that she had to do that I don't approve of. But I'm glad that she's here and all right. I intend to make it worth your while."

Drew knew Dunbar meant that he didn't approve of Melissa sleeping on the ground and guarding the two Daytons. That Drew could understand. But he felt the short hairs on the back of his neck bristle and the muscles in his jaw tighten when Dunbar mentioned making it worth his while. Scouting was his job and he'd never been bought or had anything made worth his while in all of his life and he wasn't about to start now.

"Sir," Drew tried to say in an even voice, "that won't be necessary. I'm at your party only because Miss Dunbar invited me. Not to be paid off."

"See, Papa," Melissa said, facing her father with raised eyebrows. "I told you he wasn't like the rest of my protectors."

"You never know," the senator said, patting her hand, "until you ask. I'm sorry if I insulted you, Williams. I meant no offense. Hi, John," he said to a man who'd just come in. "I'll talk to you two later."

By now the musicians were on the platform and warming up and other well-wishers were arriving. The first dance was for Melissa and the senator. Drew watched as they glided across the well-polished wooden floor. Melissa's dress floated around her like a cloud of pale green mist. Her whole face was aglow as she smiled up at her father with a radiance in her eyes. Drew didn't know what she was saying but the senator was nodding to whatever it was and smiling.

The senator was a graceful dancer and Drew wished that he was that good. But he very seldom attended the fort's few parties and didn't dance much.

Drew met the sheriff, the mayor, and several other prominent citizens. After Melissa and her father had danced around the room, the rest of the guests joined in. Sheriff Judson had introduced Drew to his daughter Sara.

She was pretty enough, with long red hair and green eyes. She was of medium height, with a square face and fair skin. Drew did think that she had too much color on her wide mouth. It looked like it was bleeding.

"I'd just love to," she purred when Drew asked her if she'd dance, batting her eyelashes at him and taking his hand.

"I understand that you and Miss Dunbar came all the way from Fort Rather together," she said suggestively, her arm around his shoulders, her fingers just touching the back of his neck.

"Well, yes, we did," Drew replied slowly, uncertain just what she meant by the statement. He didn't like the tone of her voice and the gleam in her eyes and thought that he'd better explain.

"Miss Judson . . . " he began.

"Call me Sara," she interrupted, batting her eyes up at him again.

Without calling her anything, he began once more. "I'm an army scout. Miss Dunbar wanted to be here today in time for her father's birthday. Certain circumstances made it necessary for us to travel alone." He didn't go into details about Sinclair.

Stepping back in his arm, she ran her eyes over him in an appreciative gaze.

"Are you in love with her?" she asked, looking directly into his eyes.

The question caught Drew completely off guard and he didn't have an answer ready. So he didn't say anything.

He wondered if his feelings for Melissa were so easy to read. If Sara, who'd just met him could tell so easily, then surely Melissa should know about it.

As they passed close to Melissa and an unknown distinguished-looking man, a look akin to astonishment crossed her face. Someone tapped Drew on the shoulder and in relief he thanked Sara for the dance and made his way back to the punch bowl.

Just as he raised his cup to his lips, Melissa and her partner joined him. She didn't introduce Drew to the man she'd been dancing with. But the man, looking from one to the other, saw how Melissa was staring at Drew, poured himself a glass of champagne and excused himself. They didn't even notice.

"If you have no one else to dance with," Melissa said, a pick in her voice as she smiled up at him over the rim of her punch cup, "I'd like to talk to you."

Taking a sip of punch to moisten his dry throat, Drew put the cup down and held out his arms. She stepped quickly into them, placed her hand in his and her left arm around his shoulder much in the same fashion that she'd undoubtedly seen Sara do. Her fingers just barely touched his neck.

But unlike Sara's, Melissa's touch burned deeply. Soft though her fingers were, they felt like branding irons in his hand and on his neck.

For a moment neither of them said anything. They just enjoyed the dancing. In his arms she was soft and warm and the familiar fragrance of lilacs hovered around her. Drew knew that if he never saw her again after tonight, that every time he smelled lilacs he would always remember her.

"What did you want to talk to me about?" he asked in a husky voice.

"What?" she asked, looking up at him with a soft and far-away expression in her brown eyes. "Oh, I didn't know that you could dance," she said in a whisper.

"There are several things that I can do," Drew said, grinning down at her, "besides riding a horse and throwing rocks at snakes." Drew laughed at her as she turned a brilliant red, remembering three days before. Raising her head, amusement twinkled in her eyes as her gaze met his and she laughed gaily.

"I like hearing you laugh," he said, tightening his arm around her waist. "Now what did you want to ask me?"

"Did you really mean that bringing me here was just a job?" she asked, letting herself be drawn closer to him, a pout on her pink lips.

"Well, being a scout and a guide is my job." Drew answered, seeing that she wanted to be pampered.

"But was bringing me here a job?" she insisted, stressing the word.

"Well, I will say that bringing you to Tucson," Drew said, again tightening his arm around her, bringing her still closer to him, "was one of my more pleasant jobs. It isn't every day that I get to rescue a pretty girl from a ferocious snake."

"Will you forget that snake?" she snapped, glaring up at him, a frown puckering her brows. But there was a twinkling in her eyes.

He smiled down at her and a dimple formed at the corner of her mouth. "Next question," he said.

Melissa dropped her gaze from his and again became a little flustered. "Why did you kiss me the other night?" she asked shyly, glancing up at him through thick lashes. "And this morning?"

"You mean last night, around midnight, when the rain had stopped and the stars were shining and we were in that old cabin?" he asked with a steady look and raised eyebrows. She nodded.

"Why does any man kiss a woman?" he asked, surprised at the question and frowned at her. "Haven't you ever been kissed before? Don't the men in Philadelphia know about things like that? I'll bet even Charles Sinclair, when he doesn't have his mind on that riding club in England, likes to kiss a girl."

They had reached an open window and stopped dancing for a breath of air. The room was crowded. Cigarette and cigar smoke hung over the room in a gray haze. Perfume and the heat didn't make breathing any better.

"I'm not going to answer that," she said. "Besides, I asked you a question first. A lady has a right to answer and a man should do so. That is, if you don't get beat to death by eyelashes."

Drew's heart skipped a beat as the impact of her statement dawned on him. Melissa was jealous of Sara Judson! Her eyes were flashing and her face was almost crimson.

"Okay," he said, swallowing hard, "I kissed you last night because I wanted to. Most men enjoy kissing pretty girls." Her twinkling eyes and smile told him that she was pleased with the answer.

"I kissed you this morning," he went on, "because if Dayton had gotten the drop on me, I wanted to go out with something pleasant on my mind. Did you . . . ?"

Drew wanted to ask her if she liked being kissed, but her father picked an inopportune time to join them. "Melissa, Mayor Colway's wife would like to talk to you for a few minutes."

"I'll talk to you later, Drew," she said, touching his arm and walking away only to turn and look back at him.

"More questions?" he called out.

"Could be," she answered evenly, her eyes becoming round and questioning.

"Williams," Senator Dunbar said, "I don't know how to tell you this, but I'm sure that you are partly responsible."

Drew frowned as he waited for the senator to explain himself. He had no idea what the man was talking about.

"Melissa has done nothing but talk about you since she got here," Dunbar said. "I'm surprised at the change in her. When I saw her last, she was a stubborn and willful girl. I guess I'm mostly to blame for that. But I wanted her to be aware that she's an important person."

"I guess it's all right to be important," Drew said, a twist to his lips, "but it's better to be a person first. It probably did Miss Dunbar a lot of good to rely on herself a few times instead of having someone cater to her."

The senator looked Drew up and down. He wasn't used to having someone this young, except Melissa, talk back to him without fear of recrimination. Drew gave him gaze for gaze without batting an eye.

"I don't think you're the kind of man who'd ever cater to anyone, are you, Mr. Williams?" he asked shrewdly.

"Well, I've never had to," Drew answered pleasantly, "and I don't see any reason to start now."

"Anyway, I think I like this new girl a lot

better than the other one," the senator continued. "Will you be able to stay until day after tomorrow and go back to Fort Rather with us?" he asked.

Drew knew that Melissa was behind the question. Dunbar would have his own escort and couldn't care less if Drew was along or not. A warm feeling eased over him.

"No, I'm afraid not," Drew answered. "I've got to leave in the morning. My job is through here."

"Well, if I don't see you before morning," Dunbar said, holding out his hand, "good luck and thank you."

"Thank you for the room," Drew said, shaking his hand. The senator nodded and walked away.

Drew danced with several ladies and made small talk with men he didn't know. At one point, the marshal came up to him by the window, a glass of champagne in his hand.

"What's this about Cap Dayton being killed by Chief Half Moon?" he asked. For a moment Drew wondered how the marshal had found out about it. Then he guessed that Melissa had told her father and the senator had told him. But Drew told him all of the details, which took some time.

"Why didn't you bring the Daytons and the Indians here?" the marshal asked irritably.

"For one thing," Drew replied, griped that Marshal Judson couldn't see the point, "the Indians were already heading for Fort Rather. Since they're willing to go and sign an agreement that probably won't last until the ink dries, I wasn't about to try and force them to do something that they didn't want to do and wouldn't have done anyway. And would you want your daughter to be riding with a dead man?"

"Well, you've got a point there," the marshal mused, rubbing his short chin thoughtfully.

Drew had just finished recounting to the marshal the details of Dayton's death when a shriek and a slap disrupted the party.

Looking across the room, Drew and the marshal were shocked to see Sara Judson and Melissa Dunbar going at it tooth and nail like two cats.

Right before his eyes, Drew saw Melissa draw back her right hand and let Sara have it across the left cheek. Immediately the red imprint of Melissa's hand appeared on Sara's fair skin. Sara jerked her hand to her face, her eyes blazing.

"You high-flown slut," Sara hissed and slapped Melissa across the right cheek. Both girls stood there, the print of the other's hand on her face.

"Don't you call me names, you flirt," Melissa yelled, her eyes glazed in anger and her chest rising and falling rapidly. She reached out and grabbed a hand full of Sara's red hair.

Drew came alive first and rushed toward them. A man who was standing by the window also decided that something should be done before they really hurt each other. The men reached the battling females at the same time.

Drew grabbed Melissa around the waist

and the other man did likewise with Sara and pulled them apart, each girl with a handful of the other's hair.

"What's all of this about?" Drew asked Melissa when he had her a safe distance from Sara, still holding her in his arms.

Melissa was still breathing hard and her brown eyes were almost black. Her usual desirable mouth was drawn in a tight line.

"I didn't like something she asked," Melissa answered through clenched teeth.

"What could she have asked that would make you act like this?" Senator Dunbar asked, rushing up to them.

The room fell silent waiting for her to answer. Both girls flared at the other, their chests rising and falling in heavy breathing.

"Well?" Dunbar prompted.

Melissa ducked her head in embarrassment, seemed to regain her composure, and raised her head defiantly.

"She asked just what happened between Mr. Williams and me," Melissa stated, turning red.

"Sara, what's come over you?" the sheriff asked, going to his daughter's side. Drew and the man had turned the girls loose but still stood within easy reach.

"I just wanted to see if she was as high and mighty as she appeared to be," Sara said sarcastically, a slight slur to her words. "She wouldn't even answer the question."

"The reason I didn't answer your silly question is that it's none of your business," Melissa grated, making a move toward her. Drew grabbed her arm, holding her back.

"Sara, that's enough," the sheriff said angrily. "We're invited guests and you should be ashamed of yourself. I want you to apologize."

"The only reason we were invited to this party is that you just happen to be the sheriff," Sara said unsteadily. "If we were just ordinary citizens, do you think we'd be here? We're just like those Indians. We just happen to be at the right place at the right time. If you weren't sheriff, we wouldn't be here at all.

"Sara! That will be enough," her father said, taking her by the arm and forcibly leading her from the quiet room.

"All right, folks," Senator Dunbar said nervously, trying to smile and not quite making it, "all of the excitement is over. Just a bit too much champagne."

"Are you all right?" Drew asked, looking at Melissa's disheveled hair and the red print on her face.

"Sure," she answered, an impish smile on her lips. "That was a pretty good cat fight, wasn't it? I don't see why you can't wait until day after tomorrow and go back to the fort with us," she said pensively. "You must have a girlfriend back there that you're in a hurry to see." She reached out taking his hand. Her fingers were cold.

"You sound jealous," Drew teased. "Besides, you'll be in safe hands." He tightened his fingers around hers. "This time you'll have a real guard with you and you'll probably ride in a carriage or stage. You won't have to ride a horse and . . ." Then he remembered

Tag's clothes. "You won't have to wear those old clothes either."

"But there won't be any bedrolls and shacks," she said, a twinkle replacing the sad expression in her eyes.

Suddenly the look in her eyes changed. They grew deep and soft just like the fawn's and her hand warmed in his. Still teasing, he said, "You can't have everything. Are you going back to Philadelphia with Charles Sinclair when the senator is through at Fort Rather?"

"I don't know," she answered, dropping his hand and shaking her head, the expression in her eyes changing again. "That all depends on several things and Charles Sinclair certainly isn't one of them. He's over here at my father's invitation. Not mine. Cowardliness in a man is one thing that I can't tolerate."

To Drew, listening to her talk just then, she sounded and looked like anything but a refined senator's daughter, especially with her hair hanging down around her face and Sara's hand print still vivid on her cheek.

"Just a minute ago," Drew reminded, "you were justifying to your father what Sinclair had done."

"Well, someone had to defend him," she said, "he wasn't here to do it himself. I didn't want him to look bad to Papa. What time are you leaving tomorrow?"

"Around five," he answered. "I was just about to go upstairs when that ruckus with you and Sara Judson started. I want to try and be at the fort by early day after tomorrow morning. I'm anxious to see what's happened to Half Moon and the other Daytons."

Melissa followed him out into the hall. He stood looking down at her, neither of them saying anything. Neither wanting to go. Then because he wanted to very much and because he thought she expected him to, he brushed her hair back from her face, bent down and kissed her warm mouth. He felt her lips respond beneath his this time and felt her hands at his waist. Drew slipped his arms around her waist and shoulder and pulled her tightly to him, feeling her warm body against his. Then he quickly stepped back.

"I'll see you back at the fort," he said huskily and went up the stairs without looking back. The clock in the lobby was just striking midnight.

In his room he didn't undress completely. He just took off his coat, shirt, and tie. Pulling the straight-backed chair over to the window, Drew sat down, looking out over the town.

He laughed, recalling how Melissa and Sara Judson looked slapping each other around downstairs all because of him. It was amusing that he was involved in the incident. He'd never had women fight over him.

Then he began wondering why Melissa would get into an argument with Sara over their trip in the first place. Probably just some more peculiar ways of women, he thought. But was it possible that she could be in love with him? Was it love when you didn't want to leave someone? Or someone didn't want you to leave?

He could hear the party music two floors below. The longer he sat there, the more restless he became. He knew that he should go to bed. Tomorrow would be a long and tiring day. But he really wasn't sleepy now. His mind was filled with many thoughts and all of them were of Melissa.

If she didn't care about him, she wouldn't get into a fight with another woman over him just to please herself.

Drew would like nothing better than to wait until day after tomorrow and go back to Fort Rather with Melissa and really find out what it was all about. He'd never had a woman weave her way around him like Melissa was doing and he liked it.

But he really was in a hurry to get back to the fort. Drew trusted Half Moon's word. But he also remembered Slade Dayton's promise. It was a long way to the fort and even though the Daytons were outnumbered, they weren't to be underestimated.

For a while Drew sat in the chair, his moccasined feet propped up on the window sill. The strains of a waltz drifted up to him with a calming effect. Sitting so still, with the music soft in the air, and the fragrance of lilacs still on his hands, he became drowsy. Getting up, he undressed, put the suit, white shirt and tie in the saddle bags, blew out the oil lamp, stretched out on the bed, and went to sleep.

Chapter Six

Drew's eyes opened slowly the next morning. For a moment he lay still trying to remember where he was. Afraid that he'd overslept, he rolled over and looked out the window. Seeing that it was still dark, he knew that he was still on time. Remembering the fight between Melissa and Sara Judson, he laughed.

The bed had been deceiving with the satin cover. It had been hard and the pillows were flat. Somebody had given them a good plumping to make them look so thick. But hard as the bed was, it was softer than the ground and the shack floor.

He'd carefully folded the clothes last night and put them in the saddle bags. They, he told himself a little sadly, would probably just hang in the closet at the barracks for a long time. If he did go to any of the parties at the fort, the suit would be too dressy to wear. Probably the only place he'd ever wear it would be to his own funeral and the Daytons had promised him one. Maybe to a wedding?

But now dressed in his regular clothes and

well-worn hat, he felt much more comfortable and at ease.

Drew picked up the saddle bags, pulled the door shut behind him, and went down the narrow stairs. Passing the closed dining room, he stopped, his hand on the brass door handle. He debated whether or not to go in. Why not?

Turning the handle, he stepped inside and closed the door. Moonlight streamed through the windows and illuminated the entire room, giving it a ghostly look. One of the streamers had come loose from the corner of the room and hung limply from the center of the ceiling. Most of the balloons were still hanging.

Plates, forks, and glasses littered the tables. Napkins, bottles, and cigar butts cluttered the floor. Under the window where he and Melissa had stopped to talk was a broken champagne bottle. Smoke odor hung over the room.

Must have been some party after I went upstairs, Drew said to himself while leaving the room and crossing the lobby.

Stepping out on the squeaky sidewalk, Drew shut the door behind him. It was too early to get any breakfast, so he went on to the livery stable. He'd already paid for the horses' keep, so there was no need to wake the livery man.

He saddled the horses, tied on the saddle bags and unused bedrolls, and from a bucket of water on the shelf, he filled the canteens.

It seemed that a million and one stars twinkled in the black velvet sky as Drew left the stable. The moon was slipping down behind the mountains that loomed forebodingly in the distance. A dry, crisp fragrance of sage filled the air and Drew shivered in the cold morning desert breeze. He took his buckskin jacket from the saddle bag and put it on. It felt good.

The town was sleeping quietly. There wasn't even a dog in the streets. I guess anybody with any sense at all is still sleeping, Drew thought. But if he waited until a more reasonable hour — seems like he could remember hearing someone else saying that not too long ago — he smiled at the thought of her. It would be too hot for the horses to make any time. He knew that Melissa, after a night of dancing, was sleeping soundly at the hotel.

I hope her bed is softer than mine was, Drew thought, picturing her sleeping, her arms probably spread out, not even touching the sides of the bed, not even being confined to the enveloping of the blanket. Drew had noticed that she'd kept her arms and hands, even in sleep, on the blanket, not letting them touch the ground or the floor in the shack.

But when he rode past the Burlington, Drew glanced up at the second floor where a dim light burned in the window. When he was directly under the window, a slender figure appeared. He didn't have to guess twice to know who it was. Melissa was up again at another unreasonable hour. He couldn't imagine why she'd be up at such a time, remembering the fuss she'd made three days earlier at the fort when he'd told her that they'd have to leave early.

A warm feeling swept over him as he thought

that maybe she'd gotten up just to see him off. Drew could only see her outline. Her face was obscured in the shadows. But he knew that she was looking down at him and he could imagine how she must look after seeing her at the shack. Her hair must be all tousled around her face and her eyes puffy from sleep. After looking up at her for a long minute, he raised his hand in a farewell gesture, kneed his horse in the side, and galloped down the empty street, headed southwest.

As he rode, he dozed in the saddle, slumped, his hands resting in his lap, the reins loose in his long fingers. His chin almost touched his chest.

The horse stumbled once, jarring him awake. He expected to see a bright, blazing ball of fire coming up in the east, but instead a brownish gray haze hung over everything. He'd ridden into a sandstorm!

Choking, blinding sand hung everywhere and he couldn't tell which direction was which. Everything looked the same. Drew pulled the horses to a stop. He didn't want to go back to Tucson. Not for this reason anyway. That would only be a waste of time. But if he couldn't see where he was going, it would be dangerous to go forward. They could fall into a gully or over a cliff. If he broke any bones or lost the horses, there'd be little hope for him.

No one would know where or when to begin looking for him. He'd given himself at least four days to get to Tucson and at least three back. If anything happened to him in this sand, he could be dead before a search was started.

Sandstorms were nothing new to Drew. He'd seen them many times in Texas and since he'd been out here in the Arizona Territory. But the ones he'd been in weren't this bad. Visibility was almost nothing.

Cactus that normally could be seen for miles and miles only looked like giant shadows with outstretched arms. There was nothing to give him his bearing. Usually he relied on the sun for shadows to tell the time and direction. But now that was lost and panic gripped him. He just couldn't stay where he was. He had to do something.

So dismounting and holding tightly to the reins, Drew removed his bandanna and poured water over it. He wiped his face, tied the bandanna just under his eyes, and pulled his hat down lower. Breathing was a little better. Reaching into his saddle bag, he took out an extra bandanna and poured water over it. The horse snorted and blew as Drew ran the cloth over their faces and cleaned some of the dust from their nostrils.

But then to make matters worse, the wind began blowing harder, whipping particles into his eyes. Drew gritted his teeth in order not to raise a clenched fist skyward in defiance. He had to blink his eyes several times to see.

Wrapping the reins securely around his right hand, he started walking. Slowly and carefully, very carefully, he picked his way. Time seemed to be standing still. He'd hoped to cover a lot of ground today. He wouldn't have to make as many rest stops since Melissa wasn't along. Now that seemed out of the question. He would have to go much slower.

Stumbling and staggering along, Drew guessed that he and the horses went maybe a mile in an hour. That was disgusting! He knew that he could run a mile in a lot less time. Again he felt defeated.

The ground, so far, had been pretty level. Then haste got the better of him and he increased his pace. With the dust so thick though, he couldn't see the sudden drop ahead.

Drew could feel his feet slipping, and fear of falling and seriously injuring himself or the horses gripped him. But there wasn't a thing he could do to stop his descent down the bank. Clinging desperately to the reins, the uppermost thought in his mind was keeping the horses with him. Out here, without a horse, a man was lost.

Together they spilled down the steep bank, bringing rock and sand with them. The horses screamed in terror and tried to pull the reins free. Drew tried to hold on, but the weight of the two horses pulled one of the reins out of his hand and one of the terrified animals broke free and ran.

Their descent down the bank ended with a grunt and a snort. Drew sat up, still holding the remaining reins in his right hand. It didn't hurt to take a deep breath, so evidently there were no broken ribs. He felt his arms and legs. No broken bones there either. He'd been lucky. A lesser fall could have killed him. Silently he breathed a prayer of thanks.

Then he looked at the horse, glad to see that it was his. Maybe the other horse could find his way back to the fort. While he was sitting there on the ground, he ran his hands over the animal's legs. They were all right.

Standing up, Drew looked around. They had fallen into a shallow gully. Drew was surprised that he could see for a little distance down here and the air wasn't so thick with sand.

As far as he could tell, the gully was about a hundred feet long, running up to the level ground above on the end closest to him. Back the other way, the gully was deeper. Drew led the horses back that way.

At the walled end of the gully was a hollowed-out space about ten feet wide and fifteen feet high and twenty feet deep. Drew didn't know why or how the place came to be like that. He was just awfully glad that it was there when he needed it. There was no blowing sand inside the hollow-out.

Drew tied the horse to a small bush and looked inside the hollow-out for snakes and spiders. In the back corner coiled up like a reddish brown rope was a rattlesnake. A warning sounded from the reptile as Drew approached. The deadly head lashed out and Drew jumped back. Drawing his gun, he shot the snake and the buzzing stopped.

There was nothing else to bother them, so Drew pulled the reluctant horse as far into the hollow-out as he would go. Knowing that they would probably be there for a good while, he unsaddled the horse and tied the reins to a small bush at the mouth of the hollow-out.

Taking the bandanna from his face, Drew saw that it was dry and stiff. His lips tasted like sand when he licked them. Knowing that the horse was as thirsty as he, Drew took the frying pan from the saddle bag, filled it with water, and the thirsty animal slurped down every drop.

Drew wondered how Melissa would react if she saw a horse drinking from a cooking utensil. She'd probably throw a fit and remind me to wash it when we came to the next water, he told himself with a grin.

Drew drank several cups full of water and wiped his face with the bandanna that he'd washed out. He looked around again for snakes and spiders before he sat down on the saddle to wait out the sand.

Sitting so still and with nothing to do except think about Melissa, Drew became drowsy, his eyelids getting heavy. So not to break the spell, he slid down on the ground, put his head on the saddle, pulled his hat over his face, and went to sleep.

He had no idea how long he'd slept. But a stifling, smothering feeling awakened him. The closeness of the hollow-out crowded in around him and in a panic, he flung his hat away from his face, jumped up, and almost tore his buckskin jacket off. His shirt was wringing wet and sweat trickled down his face.

Delight would be a mild description for his feelings when he ran outside. The air was as clear as any desert air he'd ever seen. All the sand was gone and only the usual desert wind was blowing.

Judging by the position of the sun, which was just about overhead, and the rumbling in his belly, it was about eleven o'clock. He had lost at least five hours!

With an oath under his breath, Drew grabbed his hat and jacket and hurried back inside the hollow-out. He gathered up the saddle and blanket and led the horse outside. When the horse was saddled, Drew took a last sip of the tepid water and found the last piece of jerky. There was also a piece of flat bread from the morning before. He started to take a bite of the bread, thought better of it, and gave it to the horse. Chewing on the jerky, he rode out of the gully. It was too hot to ride the horse very fast, so Drew sat him at a slow canter.

Miles and miles sped on. The rest had put new energy into the horse, and almost knowing that Drew was impatient to cover as much ground as possible, the animal would break into a run only to be pulled down again. They stopped once by a stream with lush green grass and the horse had a good meal.

Sand was still in Drew's hair and he could feel the grit all over him where it had penetrated through his clothes. Taking the pants and shirt that he'd worn when he and Melissa were caught in the rain, he went to the edge of the stream, undressed, and took a good bath. He didn't have any soap, but the cool water was relaxing and the scrubbing invigorating. He went all the way under the water to get the dirt from his hair.

Drew tried to imagine Charles Sinclair taking

a bath in a stream like this and the picture wouldn't take place in his mind any more than when he tried to picture Melissa in Tag's old clothes before he saw her in them.

He smiled to himself as he remembered the trouble that his mother always used to have in getting him to bathe when he was a little boy playing in the sand in Tennessee. But somehow at that age he hadn't appreciated just how good a bath could be.

After he'd bathed and put his pants on, Drew unsaddled the horse and led him into the stream. The horse seemed to know what he was supposed to do and rolled and snorted in the running water. Coming back out on the bank, he shook himself violently, sending water flying.

After he finished dressing, Drew took the coffeepot and frying pan to the stream and washed the sand out, made coffee and fresh flat bread, and opened a can of beans. A steak sure would be good, he thought. When I get back to the fort, I'm going to have Joe cook me an inch-thick steak with biscuits, gravy, and good coffee. After he'd eaten, he took the utensils back to the stream and washed them, then filled the canteens.

He rode until it was dark, and then he decided that he would try to make up the five hours that he'd lost during the sandstorm. He knew that he wouldn't get lost with the stars to guide him. It was cooler now since the sun had gone down and he let the horse run wide open for a while.

Passing the shack where he and Melissa

had stayed night before last and met the Daytons, he wished that he wasn't in such a big hurry and could spend the rest of the night there. But he wanted to get to the fort to see if the Daytons had tried anything. And he wanted to be there when Melissa arrived.

He hadn't given himself much time to think about her during the past five hours. But now that the sand was gone and the stars were out, he let her creep into his thoughts.

Melissa was a beautiful woman. She was the most, or one of the most, beautiful women he'd ever seen. There had been a girl in New Orleans, Michelle Dousette, two years ago that Drew could never forget if he lived to be a hundred. Black hair, big brown eyes, and soft olive skin. Red alluring lips that could promise a man anything. But she'd wanted him to stay in New Orleans and he'd wanted to go West. Neither of them would give in to the other. Michelle was another time and another place. This was now and Melissa was on his mind. He'd never met anyone quite like her before.

But I guess when you're used to being pampered and getting your own way, it's hard to change, Drew thought as he galloped along. I know I wouldn't want to change my way of life for one like hers.

He'd never have believed that he'd ever see the day when a woman of Melissa's standing would be holding a gun on two dangerous men that had threatened to kidnap her.

Drew grinned when he remembered the commotion she'd made about always wearing a dress and then having to spend a night and day in someone else's clothes. Neither did he believe that he'd ever kiss a girl like Melissa or have a girl like her almost beg him to kiss her again. But I guess life has its funny sides, too.

He still thought it was hilarious the way she and Sara Judson were calling each other names and slapping one another's face until they were red and trying to pull the other's hair out by the roots. And all because of him!

Drew felt a little giddy just thinking about her. A warm feeling started in his toes and worked its way slowly up to his head, lingering around his heart and in the middle of his stomach. Even in the dry air he could still smell the lilacs. He looked down at his hands and could feel her small warm hand on his. Pushing his hat back on his head, he sighed deeply, thinking how soft and warm her lips had been when he'd kissed her last night.

But he knew that he was only indulging himself in daydreams. He had nothing to offer a girl like Melissa. She was used to three square meals a day and all of them on time and much more than bread, jerky, and beans cooked in one skillet. This was probably the first time in her life she'd ever had to eat from utensils other than china and crystal and served by an army scout instead of a butler or maid, out in the middle of nowhere. She probably slept on satin sheets in a big poster bed instead of a bedroll, and a carriage was no doubt her usual means of travel.

How do I know that she'd want me to offer her anything? he asked himself. She could have been going along with all those things and leading him on just to amuse herself. Men never knew how a woman's mind operated.

I guess that ever since time began, women have been a puzzle to men, Drew thought. But if she hadn't been interested in him, why was she so insistent that he wait until tomorrow and go back to the fort with them?

And why did she ask so many questions? How he felt about taking care of her? And saying that there wouldn't be any shack to sleep in on the way back with her father? And why had he kissed her? And why had she seemed so jealous of Sara Judson? And why had she gotten up so early?

Drew didn't know what Melissa's answers to those questions would be. But he liked his own answers. And his answer was that she was really interested in him.

Letting his mind wander ahead to the point where things between them were such that he'd have to change jobs, Drew wondered what else he could do except be an army scout.

Even if he remained single, he couldn't be a scout the rest of his life. He knew a little about cattle and wouldn't mind owning a small ranch. Small at first, of course. Then expand.

He wouldn't want to stay in Arizona if he had a family. It would be too hot for Melissa. She'd probably insist on living back East. But on that he would refuse. He couldn't stand the big cities and the way they dressed and talked. Texas. Texas would be a good place for a ranch.

Would Melissa consider being a rancher's wife? She'd said that she'd be a scout's wife, depending on who the scout was. The look in her eyes, when she'd said that, gave him reason to believe that she would go anywhere with him.

I'll try to find out a few of these answers when I see her. But what if she goes back to Philadelphia before I see her again? It'll be my luck for Walters to send me out on a job and she'll be gone.

The horse's foot hit a rock and he stumbled a little, bringing Drew's thoughts back to the present.

The night air was velvet cool and the horse was still running easy. But there was no need in killing him. Drew pulled the animal to a stop and they rested for a short while.

Drew had always liked the desert at night. It had a peacefulness to it. The stars were twinkling like diamonds on black velvet, and the moon was up, hanging like a yellow ball in the sky. A coyote bayed mournfully somewhere in the hills and an owl, perched on the out-stretched arm of a cactus, let out a bone-chilling screech.

Drew and the horse started out once again. This time Drew let the horse pick its own pace and that was a fast gallop. Drew wasn't sleepy now. There was too much on his mind to think about sleep now.

I wonder what Slade and Tom Dayton have done? I know if they get the chance, they'll try to escape from Half Moon or kill him.

If I wore the Dayton boots, I sure wouldn't

try anything with so many men around me, Drew thought. Especially since the Indians didn't hesitate to shoot one man being so well armed as Cap Dayton had been. Even the fact that they'd done business together hadn't stopped them from killing him. I'd at least wait until I was in the guardhouse.

In any event, he knew that the Daytons just wouldn't sit still and do nothing. When the senator signed that agreement with the Indians and they had to stop killing the buffalo just for the hides, it would mean an end to the Daytons' easy money and they wouldn't give up so easy. If Half Moon was dead and couldn't sign the agreement, the Daytons could get away from the other Indians and over into Mexico before anything else could happen.

Drew knew that he and the horse were making good time. He was covering much more ground alone than he would have if Melissa had been with him. The minutes had slipped into hours and the miles passed beneath the horse's flying feet.

Coming to a stream, with an abundance of grass, Drew decided to stop and really sleep for a while. He unsaddled the horse and hobbled him near a clump of grass. Taking the saddle bags, he dropped them on the ground by the saddle. Spreading the blankets on the ground, he was dumbfounded, to say the least, to see Melissa's blue dress and a small white handkerchief folded up.

He hadn't opened the bedrolls since they left the shack and he must have given Melissa the wrong one. No wonder she had on that green dress last night. He'd had the other one! Wonder where she'd gotten the green one? It didn't look like the kind of dress that would come from Oppenheimer's. That one, like this, had been made for her.

He stood staring down at the dress on the blanket for a full minute. He laughed out loud as he bent down, picked up the dress and handkerchief, and clumsily folded and put them in the other saddle bag with his own clothes. Maybe someday we can pack our clothes together.

Wonder why she didn't mention it? he questioned as he stretched out on the lilac-scented blanket. Maybe she thought that it would have embarrassed him. And it would have. Even now he felt a little foolish. He did wish, though, that he could have seen her face when she realized that she didn't have a dress to wear. Folding his arms under his head, Drew drifted off to sleep with the fragrance of lilacs around him and dreamed of Melissa.

They were still at the shack. But she was wearing the green dress instead of Tag's old pants and shirt. The same musicians who'd played for the senator's party were playing just for them. Only he and Melissa were dancing. His steps were as smooth as the senator's and he held her close in his arms. She looked up at him as though he was the only one in the world for her.

Sunshine, peeping over the mountains, awakened him. There were a few clouds in the blue sky and the birds were singing. It was going to be a nice day. The horse was contentedly munching on the green grass by the stream where Drew hobbled him last night.

Jumping up, he discovered that he was sore from his fall down the cliff yesterday. Bending over a couple of times, he touched his toes and then stretched his arms over his head, relieving the soreness some. Then jerking the bedroll together, Drew threw the saddle on the horse and took off.

The desert was beautiful at this time of morning. Gold, red, and pearl of sunrise. Purple mountains in the far distance. Brown hills and the yellow, pink, and white flowers. An eagle soared majestically high above.

Fort Rather finally came into view around noon. Drew rode through the gate and thought he'd never seen a place look so good. But his joy was short-lived.

No sooner had he turned his horse into the corral than he heard his name called. Only this time it wasn't by the private.

"Williams, I want to talk to you in my office immediately," Colonel Walters bellowed, running behind him. Drew had never seen him so angry. Walters looked like he was about to have a fit. Looking down at the colonel, Drew became disturbed at the tone in his voice.

If he didn't calm down, Walters would have a stroke.

Red spots stood out on his fair face like rouge on a circus clown's face. He was breathing hard through his nose like he'd been running. And run was something that Walters never did. If the distance to be covered wasn't too far, he'd walk. But if walking was out of the distance, he rode a horse or in some kind of carriage.

"Will you unsaddle my horse and take my things to the barracks, Jimmy?" Drew asked a young private who was throwing hay to the horses in the corral.

The young man began doing as he was asked as Drew and the colonel walked away.

"What's the matter?" Drew asked, shortening his stride as he walked along beside the colonel, perplexed at the man's actions.

"I'll tell you in my office," Walters said evenly, walking as fast as his short legs could carry him. When they were inside, the colonel hurried around the cluttered desk and plopped down in his swivel chair. Once again the smothering feeling engulfed Drew in the crowded office. He sat down in the chair, crossing his long legs at the ankles.

"Now, what's the matter?" Drew asked in a gentle tone, hoping to calm the colonel. In the two years he'd been at the fort, he'd never seen the colonel like this.

"What in the world did you mean letting the Daytons come back here with Half Moon?" Walters roared, leaning forward and gripping the edge of the desk.

"That should be obvious," Drew said softly, trying not to lose his temper. "My job, if you remember, was to take Melissa Dunbar and Charles Sinclair to Tucson. I couldn't bring her all the way back here if she was going to be there in time for her father's party. I certainly couldn't take the Daytons to Tucson with a dead man tied to a horse and Miss Dunbar along. There was no other choice. The Daytons are here, aren't they? And Half Moon? What are you so mad about?"

Slamming his fist violently down against the desk and wincing in pain, Walters sprang to his feet, breathing hard between clenched teeth. His blue eyes were blazing behind his glasses.

"I'll tell you what I'm so mad about," he shouted, rubbing his fingers. "Slade Dayton shot Half Moon yesterday!"

"Shot Half Moon?" Drew repeated, jumping to his feet, his throat contracting. He could feel the sweat oozing from every pore in his body and his mouth went dry. The hair on the back of his neck seemed to be standing straight up and his breath left him. "Is he dead?" Drew asked, finally finding his voice.

"No," the colonel answered slowly, glaring at him. "He's not dead."

"How could Dayton shoot Half Moon?" Drew asked, a bewildered frown puckering his forehead. "The Daytons' hands were tied behind them."

"The way Little Bear tells it," the colonel explained in short breaths, "they stopped to eat at Cottonwood Creek Crossing and Tom and Slade conned Half Moon into untying them. Somehow Slade got to his saddle bag where he had an extra gun. Why didn't you search their belongings?"

Drew shrugged his shoulders. "I just didn't think anything would happen with the Daytons tied and so many men around them. How bad is Half Moon?"

"The doctor says he'll be all right," the colonel said, sitting down in the chair, calming a little. "He was only shot in the left arm. But we may have lost the chance of getting him to sign the agreement with Dunbar. He said he'd come here in good faith and he'd given you his word that nothing would happen to the Daytons."

"I know he gave his word," Drew said, raising his voice. "But I didn't promise him that the Daytons wouldn't try to escape. He should have known they would. He'd have done the same thing. What happened to Slade?" Drew asked. He didn't feel guilty about Half Moon and Slade Dayton. Melissa Dunbar had been his prime responsibility and he'd gotten her safely to her father with only a few complications.

But a thought had begun building in the back of Drew's mind and if Walters' brain worked in its usual channels, that thought was about to become a reality.

"Slade escaped," Walters said slowly, his blue eyes becoming slits. Little Bear and his men were able to hang on to Tom and bring him and Half Moon back here. But somebody has to go after Slade and bring him back." Walters turned his head, giving Drew a sideways look.

There it was, Drew told himself. That same gleam sparkled in Walters' eyes now as it did when he told Drew about Melissa. Drew didn't offer to go after Slade. He knew Walters would get pleasure from almost ordering him to go.

"Since you were so successful in getting

Melissa Dunbar to her father," Walters said with a sneer, "you should have no trouble in tracking Dayton." Walters leaned back in his chair and folded his hands across his rotund belly.

"Colonel," Drew began plaintively and standing up, "I've been in the saddle for the past five days. Let one of your glory-hungry sergeants take a patrol out and earn their pay."

"Williams, you know as well as I do that Dayton could spot a patrol a mile away. One man stands a better chance in going after him and bringing him back." The colonel looked very pleased with himself knowing that his word would be final.

Knowing that it would do no good to argue, Drew asked, "Where did Half Moon lose Dayton and how soon do I start?"

"The sooner you start, the sooner you'll be back," Walters said philosophically. "I told you that Dayton got away at Cottonwood Creek Crossing."

That's where Drew had spent part of last night! Cold chills ran up and down his back. He remembered Slade's promise before they left the shack. Wonder why he didn't try to jump me last night? Drew asked himself.

"What happened to Tom Dayton?" Drew asked.

"I told you that, too," Walters replied irritably. "Half Moon's men hung on to him." Walters stood up, again silently envying this job that Drew was about to do. "He's in the guardhouse."

Drew knew that it would be useless and a

waste of time to argue with Walters when his mind was already made up about him going after Slade. But Drew was disappointed and a little angry that he wouldn't be at the fort when Melissa arrived. "I'm going to get a few hours' sleep," Drew told Walters. "A few extra hours won't matter," he hurriedly added when he saw that Walters was going to interrupt. "Dayton won't go too far," Drew continued. "He promised the other day that he'd get me. He holds me responsible for Cap's death."

"In case you're interested," Walters called out as Drew reached the door, "that English fellow, Sinclair, got back here day before yesterday on a stage. Poor devil was scared to death."

Drew had completely forgotten about Charles Sinclair. He'd had more important things on his mind than the Englishman. The sand storm for one thing and, of course, there was Melissa.

"Did he bring the horse back with him?" Drew asked.

"Yes," Walters replied. "It was tied to the stage. He even remembered to return my hat."

Before the colonel could launch into some reminiscences about the hat, Drew left the office, slamming the door shut behind him. The corporal looked up from the paperwork on the desk before him. Drew didn't usually show such bursts of temper.

"I guess you don't need to be told how out of sorts he was?" the corporal asked, nodding toward the colonel's door. "After Half Moon and his braves and the Daytons got here, he ranted and raved about how he could have done a better job."

"Maybe in his younger days he could have," Drew replied. "By the way. What did they do with Cap Dayton's body?"

"Oh, they buried him out behind the fort," the corporal said easily. "Are you goin' after Slade by yourself?"

"Yeah," Drew replied dryly. "I really don't see why Walters has an army here. All he needs is you, himself, and me." The corporal leaned back in his chair and laughed at the silly suggestion.

"Well, good luck to you, Mr. Williams," he said, still grinning. "I'm glad that I'm not in your shoes."

"I don't suppose you'd want to trade jobs with me this time, would you?" Drew asked with raised eyebrows.

"No, sir," the corporal replied, shaking his head slowly. "Not for all the money in the world. There was only a fifty-fifty chance that you'd get killed the other time. Now it's just about ninety to ten in favor of Dayton."

"Thanks a lot for the confidence," Drew said with a half smile. The corporal raised his right hand in a salute. Drew nodded his head and left.

Walking toward the barracks, Drew heard Tag call him. "I reckon you're goin' after Dayton, huh?" Tag asked, an expectancy in his eyes.

"Yep," Drew answered simply, knowing what the youngster had in mind and remembering his promise to him.

"You promised I could go with you next time," Tag said slowly, holding Drew's gaze.

"Can you use a gun?" Drew asked. He wasn't happy about the situation, but he'd never gone back on his word before. He felt trapped by his hasty promise.

Tag nodded slowly. Drew didn't know how much of the truth he was telling.

"Do you realize you can get yourself killed on something like this?" Drew asked, looking straight into Tag's green eyes.

Again Tag nodded. This time with a swallow and more slowly.

"Okay," Drew agreed. "Go tell Colonel Walters I said you were going with me and that it's your idea. Then get yourself a good horse and plenty of ammunition. We'll leave in about two hours."

"Two hours?" Tag repeated wide-eyed and impatiently, turning around to face Drew. "What are you gonna do now? Shouldn't we leave right away?"

"I'm going to get a couple of hours' sleep," Drew said calmly, as though he did this kind of thing every day. "Dayton will wait."

"Oh," Tag said smiling at him. There was a spring in the boy's steps as he hurried away in the direction of Walters' office. Drew just shook his head as he went toward the barracks and a few hours' rest. If that kid only knew what he's getting into.

Drew found his saddle bags and bedroll on his bunk in the barracks. Just as he started to unload the contents, Charles Sinclair came in.

"Williams, I didn't get a chance to talk to you before you went into Colonel Walters' office," he said, twirling the riding crop in his fingers. "But I just wanted to know whether Senator Dunbar was very angry with me for not arriving in Tucson with you and Melissa."

"If he could have gotten his hands on you, Sinclair," Drew said with a cold look in his eyes, "he'd have skinned you alive. That's how upset he was. Especially when he found out that Melissa had to guard two of the Daytons by herself while I went after Cap."

"What do you mean? Melissa guarding two of the Daytons?" Sinclair asked, his eyes almost falling out of his head.

"The Daytons found us in a shack," Drew explained, "and Cap was going to take her ring to Senator Dunbar. On his way to Tucson, one of Half Moon's men killed him. I started out after Cap, so naturally Miss Dunbar had to stay at the shack to guard the other men. That really burned the senator up."

Sinclair batted his eyes a couple of times and shifted his weight from one foot to the other. Drew, forgetting about the dress in his saddle bags, dumped the contents out on the bed. Naturally Sinclair saw the dress first.

"Well, really," Sinclair exclaimed regaining his composure. "Just how are you going to explain that?" he asked, pointing the riding crop toward the crumpled dress.

"I don't have to explain a thing to you, Sinclair," Drew said on the verge of drawing back his fist. "So you'd better take yourself some place else. I've got another job to do and

I need some rest." The Englishman started toward the door. "Sinclair," Drew called after him. His hand on the doorknob, Sinclair turned to face Drew who said, "I don't want to hear a word, not one, about this," pointing toward the dress on the bed.

"Well, really," Sinclair muttered as he hurried out the door, slamming it behind him.

The question of what to do with the dress popped into Drew's mind. He couldn't hide it in the closet. Somebody would see it there. So quickly before anyone came in, he folded the dress up more carefully this time, stuffed it back into the saddle bags, and shoved it under his bunk.

Chapter Seven

Drew didn't go to sleep after Sinclair left the barracks. He just stretched out on the bunk and rested a few minutes. It wasn't even two when he got up, put on a fresh shirt, and went outside. He didn't have to go to the corral for his horse. Tag was waiting for him with two fresh horses already saddled. They mounted and rode toward the gate.

"Tag, what did Colonel Walters say when you told him you were going with me after Dayton?" Drew inquired as they rode away from the fort.

"He called me a crazy young fool," Tag answered with a happy grin on his thin face and Drew couldn't help noticing the eager look of anticipation in his green eyes. "He also said that I'd end up gettin' myself killed followin' you."

"He could be right, you know?" Drew said, with raised eyebrows, glancing at the adventure-seeking youth riding beside him. He could hardly keep from laughing at the way Tag was dressed. He looked like he was heading for a revolution.

When Drew had told Tag to get plenty of ammunition, he only meant enough shells for a pistol and a rifle. But he hadn't expected anything like this.

Around Tag's lean waist was strapped a gun belt with all of the notches filled. There was a Smith & Wesson .44 tied down at the right thigh. Two cartridge belts with all the notches filled were crossed over his thin chest and a rifle was stuck down in a well-worn scabbard.

"I hope you don't have to run with all of that stuff on," Drew said as they galloped along. "If you do, you'll break your neck."

"I just want to be ready for Dayton," Tag answered, blushing.

"Tag, you're ready for a war," Drew laughed, wondering where Tag had gotten the clothes he was wearing. He was surprised at them as he was at the amount of ammunition Tag carried. They were so out of character for him, being almost new.

The light blue shirt was buttoned so close around Tag's neck that he looked like he'd choke. The legs of the virtually new navy blue pants were stuffed down into polished black boots. Tag's old floppy and battered campaign hat rested nonchalantly on the back of his blond head.

"Tag, where did you get those clothes?" Drew asked, unable to contain his curiosity.

"Oh, I've had 'em for a long time," Tag replied, riding loose in the saddle, the reins in a light grip in his long fingers, "I've been savin' 'em for a special occasion."

"You call going out looking for outlaws a 'special occasion'?" Drew asked, staring at the boy.

"Well, it's more than I've ever done before," Tag answered a little pensively, pulling his hat down to shade his eyes from the afternoon sun.

"Tag, why did you want to come on a thing like this?" Drew asked as they rode along. He knew that the question was silly. He could remember when he was young and wanted to do something exciting and dangerous. But not to the point of getting killed.

But now that he was older and had been in a war and had chased outlaws and guided wagon trains through some pretty dangerous country, he was almost ready to find a steady job and settle down. Especially now that he'd met Melissa. That idea seemed pretty good.

"Well, because I wanted to," Tag replied simply, as if that was answer enough, and he looked at Drew as though he was surprised that he would have to ask such a question. "I guess I wanted to prove to myself and a lot of others that I can do something besides mend saddles and feed horses."

"Don't you think that you could find a little safer way to prove yourself than going out to find a man that you might end up killing?" Drew asked. "And like the colonel said, you could get killed. Why haven't you joined the troops? You look old enough."

"Well, if I was in the army, I sure wouldn't be here," Tag answered resolutely. "Colonel Walters wouldn't send a patrol after Dayton.

So this is the only way that I could go with you."

Drew watched the expression on Tag's face change from petulance to excitement again.

"Where are we gonna find Dayton?" Tag asked, impatience in his voice. Drew had the feeling that Tag wanted to change the subject from himself.

"Colonel Walters said that Half Moon told him that Dayton jumped them at Cottonwood Creek Crossing," Drew answered. "He has a good start on us. But he promised the other day that he'd get me. So he may not have gone too far since he knew that I was taking Miss Dunbar to Tucson and would be back in a few days."

"Get you?" Tag asked, twisting around in the saddle to face Drew, his face turning white. "For what? What do you mean? I thought you were just going after Dayton because you're a scout."

Drew told Tag, sparing none of the details. He told him about Chief Half Moon overtaking Cap Dayton on his way to Tucson with Melissa's ring and about Cap killing one of Half Moon's men. Then about Little Bear killing Cap Daton. About Melissa guarding Tom and Slade at the shack and Slade promising to make Drew pay for Cap's death. Drew watched the expression change on Tag's face again. Change from wide-eyed disbelief to open-mouthed excitement.

"Golly, Ned," the boy drawled out in a shout. "Man, I wish I could've been there to see all of that. If you'd let me gone with you at first," Tag chided, "I could've brought the Daytons back without anything happening."

"This trip might be just as exciting, Tag," Drew promised with a nod.

"Why?" Tag asked, his eyes wide.

"Because Slade Dayton promised to kill me," Drew said bluntly. "And he meant it. One of us will die today."

Tag's green eyes met Drew's for a second, then he dropped his gaze down to his hands and he didn't say anything else.

It was about three when they reached Cottonwood Creek Crossing. The creek ran north and south with the road crossing east and west. Shaded by cottonwood trees, a plank bridge, just wide enough to accommodate a stage or a large wagon, spanned the creek. There was no way to tell which of the many tracks around the bridge were Dayton's. They went every direction, and some time had passed.

"Which way do you think he went, Drew?" Tag asked when they'd stopped under the shade of a cottonwood tree by the bridge. There was apprehension in the boy's eyes as he looked around the area and finally at Drew.

Tag's right hand gripped the handle of his pistol so hard that his knuckles turned white. Drew, without asking, knew the boy was scared.

"I was just going to ask you the same thing," Drew replied, looking around the hills and gullies. Any place was perfect for an ambush if that's what Dayton had in mind.

"Me?" Tag asked astonished, his voice breaking and his eyes wide in disbelief.

"Sure," Drew said. "You didn't think you were just coming along for the ride, did you? You're keen and perceptive." Drew was surprised that the boy had so little self-confidence.

"If you were a fugitive with a grudge," Drew asked, "and you managed to escape from your captors, where would you hide if you didn't know exactly when the person you wanted would return?"

"Well," Tag drawled, shoving his hat back on his head and scratching his chin, "I'd try to find a place close to water and close to the fort. You are talkin' about you, ain't you?"

Drew nodded in answer to the question.

"Half Moon said that Dayton jumped them here at the bridge when they had stopped to eat," Drew said after a moment. "That was three days ago. If Dayton's been watching the fort, he knows that I'm back and he's probably been following us."

Drew saw Tag swallow hard and lick his lips. He knew that Tag was getting scared at being followed by a killer and he was sorry that he'd let the boy talk him into letting him come along on such a dangerous thing. If anything happens to the boy, he would be responsible and would never hear the end of it from Walters.

"Tag, do you want to go back to the fort?" Drew asked, searching the boy's face, wishing that he would say yes. This job would be so much easier on Drew if he didn't have to worry about Tag. This was no place for a boy who'd never done more than mend a saddle or pitch hay to horses.

Just for a brief moment, Drew thought that Tag was going to agree and go back. But the boy only swallowed hard and, seeming to summon up all of the courage of his youth, said, "Gosh, no! This is the most exciting day in my entire life, Drew. I wouldn't go back to the fort for anything. Only if you make me." There was a pleading in his eyes.

"Okay," Drew said, reaching out and slapping the boy on the shoulder. "Let's not waste any more time then. We didn't pass any shacks on the way we came. So let's head northeast. That's still between the fort and the creek."

They started out again, Drew leading the way with Tag only a few paces behind him. Drew remembered seeing an old abandoned shack out this way two months ago when he'd had a few days off and had gone hunting.

The shack was about a mile from Cottonwood Creek Crossing. Up one hill. Down a hill. Around one bend. Then another. Any one of them would have been an excellent place to wait for someone.

The sun beat down on them relentlessly and sweat stained their clothes. There was hardly a breath of air and what little there was felt like it was searing their lungs as they breathed.

"If I was Dayton," Drew said over his shoulder to Tag, "I wouldn't waste too much time."

"Why be in such a hurry?" Tag asked, riding up beside Drew.

"Well, the sooner the job is done, the sooner

he can be on his way to Mexico," Drew said with candor.

"Why would he want to go to Mexico?" Tag asked, squinting his eyes in the sun as he frowned at Drew.

"Well, I'm sure that the Daytons have a good bit of money saved," Drew answered, "and since Cap's dead and Tom's in the guardhouse, Slade could live like a king down there. There are no extradition agreements between the United States and Mexico. That means the sheriff couldn't bring him back." Then Tag nodded, understanding what Drew was talking about.

Riding out of a ravine and topping a hill, they saw the shack below. It was a small building with a shingled roof and quite a few of them missing. There was a clearing on three sides of the building and rocky hills in the back. From their vantage point, they could see one door in the front and one window on the west side of the shack. There were no trees around it and only a sparse amount of grass grew from the rocks.

Tag and Drew rode as close to the shack as they dared without losing the protection of the few trees they were in. They dismounted and tied the horses to a scrub tree. There was a boulder some twenty feet from the tree. So bending low they ran the distance and dropped down on the ground.

The afternoon sun beat down on them in reprimand for being there. Sweat ran down their backs and Drew saw Tag reach up and unbutton his shirt collar and wipe sweat from his forehead with the back of his hand. But Tag made no comment as he shoved his hat back on his head.

If Dayton had been in the shack, he could have picked them both off without any trouble at all. There was about fifty yards between the shack and the boulder they were crouching behind with nothing at all in between for protection.

Crouching there, Drew said, "Well, Tag, I guess the only way to get down there is to get down there. I'm positive, though, that Dayton's not in the shack."

"Why?" Tag asked, frowning and breathing hard, the sweat still running down his young face. "Where else would he be?"

"It's simple, Tag," Drew replied, irritation edging his voice. "If Dayton was down there, we certainly wouldn't be here. He could've seen us coming. It was completely open between those scrub trees where the horses are and here to this boulder. Unless," he went on, thoughtfully rubbing his chin, "he wants to catch us between here and the shack, then let us have it."

They crouched there a few minutes longer. The only sounds, other than Tag's breathing, were the wind and the birds. Finally, expelling a deep breath, Drew stood up.

"Let's go, Tag," he said. "We've waited long enough." Tag stood up. But as if to delay longer, he made a big production of checking his pistol and ammunition belts.

"Tag," Drew said, looking at him apprehensively, "If you're going to try to run with all that ammunition on, you'll never make it. Why don't you take off those cross belts and just put some shells in your pocket? Your rifle and pistol will be enough."

"That's a good idea," Tag said, looking grateful for the delay.

Drew stepped from around the protection of the boulder and Tag followed him. "Just bend low and run," Drew said to Tag over his shoulder. "You take the right side of the shack and I'll take the left."

Bending as low as they could and still run, they raced across the clearing without any trouble. Drew was really surprised that Dayton hadn't tried to get them as they ran across the open space. That's what he'd have done if he'd been Dayton. He and Tag reached the rickety porch and hit the door at the same time.

Leaning against the wall of the weather-beaten shack, they listened for sounds from inside. Nothing. Drew then stepped back and kicked the door. It burst open on its rusty hinges and part of the latch slammed to the floor on the other side.

Inside they saw that the shack had only one room, and with a single glance around, it was easy to see that no one was there now.

There was no place to hide with just a table, two chairs, and a small stove as the only furnishings. A shovel lay in one corner.

But there were signs that someone had spent at least one night there. An unmade bedroll and the remnants of a meal were on the floor; a hunk of bread, a piece of bacon, and a half cup of coffee were still on the table. Dayton must have been eating, heard them coming, and run.

"Well, it's plain to see he's not here," Drew said to Tag who was standing just inside the door. Drew got the uneasy feeling, which years of experience had given him, that they were being watched. The hairs on the back of his neck felt like they were giving signals and an icy feeling ran up and down his back.

Dayton couldn't be too far away. He was probably crouching down behind a cactus or a boulder as Drew and Tag had been only a few minutes ago, just waiting for the right moment.

Another quick glance around the single room showed that one small window was the only other way out of the shack.

"Well, Tag," Drew said with a half smile and raised eyebrows, "it's now or never. We'll try going out the door first, although I'm sure that Dayton has that covered now."

Drew felt sorry for Tag again, seeing the color drain from his face. Then the youngster swallowed and seemed to regain himself.

"If we can't get out the door, Drew," Tag said, a confidence in his voice that Drew hadn't heard before, "we can crawl out that little window." Tag pointed to the window at the west end of the room.

"You've got a point there, Tag," Drew said, pretending that he hadn't thought of the window as a means of escape. A bright smile lit up Tag's green eyes.

Drew stepped over behind the door and

opened it. A bullet slammed into the door, hitting just about where his head would have been, quickly followed by a second shot about eight inches further down. Tag reached out and slammed the door shut much faster than Drew had opened it.

"Well, at least we know where he is," Tag said, expelling a deep breath. Up until now, Tag hadn't drawn his gun. But he jerked the pistol from his holster, opened the door just a crack big enough for the barrel to stick through, and fired two quick shots.

He slammed the door shut again just in time to hear the splat of a bullet in the weather-beaten lumber.

"Staying in here won't get the job done, Tag," Drew said, walking toward the window. "We've got to get out of here. So I guess we'll have to use the window like you said."

The window had been meant for light and a small amount of that. It only had four small panes and couldn't be raised. Getting out of it probably hadn't occurred to the builders.

Taking the bandanna from around his neck and putting on his gloves, Drew held the handkerchief up over the top pane and with the butt of the gun, tapped it just hard enough to crack it. He didn't want Dayton to hear glass shattering and sneak down and pick them off as they climbed through the window.

With his buckskin gloves on, it was easy to pull the cracked glass, then the small pieces of wood and the other panes out. When he was finished, he turned around to find Tag watching him, an expression of awe on his face.

"You must know how to do everything," Tag said softly and enviously.

"When you do this kind of work, Tag," Drew replied matter-of-factly and without boasting, "you've got to be one step ahead all of the time or you won't step ahead any more." Drew returned the bandanna to his pocket after shaking the glass out.

Taking the chair to the window, Drew turned around to face Tag. "Do you want to go first?" he asked.

Tag nodded eagerly and started to step up on the chair, his rifle in his hand.

"Tag," Drew said quickly, "this is a bad time for a lesson. But don't ever crawl through a small place with a loaded gun in your hand. Either holster it, push it in front of you, or give it to someone. Let me have it."

Tag spun around and handed Drew the rifle. With his thin size, he had no trouble at all as he quickly crawled through the window and dropped the few feet to the ground. His foot hit a rock and he fell to the ground on his back with a grunt.

Standing up, he took the rifle from Drew, who had a harder time squeezing his broad shoulders through the narrow space. But he managed to wiggle through and dropped down beside Tag.

They were out of sight, to the west, from where Dayton's last shot had come. Walking around behind the shack, they found where a horse was tied and footprints went around the other side of the shack and disappeared up into the rocks.

Dayton hadn't fired at them since he and Tag had exchanged shots a few minutes ago. But he was still out there. Drew was sure of it. He took Tag's rifle and put his hat on the barrel, sticking just the edge of it around the corner of the shack.

Instantly a shot rang out, echoing through the hills and rocks. Drew's hat sailed off the barrel and settled in the dust, a hole in the crown. Drew pulled the hat to him, picked it up, and stuck his finger through the new puncture.

"I'd say he's a pretty good shot," Tag said, his thumbs hooked in his belt.

Drew nodded and looked up at the sky. They wouldn't have much more time to do anything before night if they didn't hurry. He didn't want to be out in these mountains and hills after dark with Tag to worry about if he still hadn't caught Dayton.

"Our only safe way to get to him is to drop back here behind the shack, get into the rocks, and then circle around to him," Drew said.

"Shouldn't we go in different directions?" Tag suggested. There wasn't much conviction in his voice and Drew knew that he was only saying it to sound helpful.

"We should," Drew agreed. "But since this is your first time at something like this, we'll stay together. Are you ready?"

Tag nodded and looked a little relieved that Drew didn't go along with his suggestions.

They walked away from the back of the shack, keeping it between them and where the lasts shots were fired. Putting at least twenty yards of rock and cactus between them and the shack, Drew and Tag began circling east.

"Drew, while we're slipping around to this side of Dayton, is he stupid enough to just sit and wait for us to find him?" Tag asked as they climbed through the rocks.

"No, he isn't stupid, Tag," Drew answered, surprised again at Tag's perceptiveness. "He knows we're after him because he's been waiting for us."

Drew saw a sick look pass over Tag's face and knew that the boy's life had never been threatened before. "I mean that he's after me. But he won't know which way we're coming from."

"No, he won't," Tag said as he climbed behind Drew. "But we won't know where he is either."

They were high enough now for a good view of the area below. The shack look so desolate down there. The horses were still tied where they'd been left, and still more and more of the seemingly never ending desert and mountains spread out around them. But there was no trace of Dayton.

"He must have seen us moving around here in the rocks," Drew said, searching around. "Let's move a little further up."

They hadn't gone too far when Tag suddenly reached out and grabbed Drew's arm, pulling him down with him on the ground.

"I just saw a flash up there to the right," Tag said, pointing toward a clump of rocks higher up than they were. "It could be the sun on a rifle barrel," Tag continued, to the frown on Drew's face. Just then a shot rang out and zinged off a rock just in front of Drew.

Drew frowned because he prided himself on being aware of details and on being on the lookout for small things. Now here was a kid, who'd never been involved in a thing like this before, seeing what his keen and trained eyes had missed.

"Do you want . . . ?" Tag started to ask when a second shot sounded and resounded among the rocks. The sound startled a bunch of wren that had built a nest in a nearby cactus and in a flurry, wings flew away.

Drew heard Tag gasp and groan. Spinning around in his bent-over position, Drew saw Tag grasping his right thigh in both hands, blood beginning to stain his pants. The boy's face was as white as the clouds above and he looked as if he'd faint.

Drew shoved his pistol into the holster and helped Tag sit down on the ground and leaned him back against a rock, straightening his legs out in front of him.

Tag gasped and his arms went limp, his hands falling away from his leg. Drew thought that Tag had fainted, but the boy was just weak from the shock of being shot.

Drawing the long knife from a sheath on his boot, Drew slit Tag's pants leg all the way up to the thigh. The bullet had entered the right side of Tag's leg just above the knee and had gone all the way through. The oozing blood made it look a lot worse than it really was.

"Well, at least we know where he is or was,"

Tag said, opening his green eyes and giving Drew a tight-lipped smile. Drew returned the smile as he reached out and took the handkerchief from Tag's pocket and quickly tied it around the upper part of the boy's leg.

"You'll be all right, Tag," Drew said, patting him on the shoulder, trying to reassure him. He handed him the rifle, saying, "The bullet went all the way through and there are no broken bones. I'm going after Dayton now. Maybe he'll take more chances with one of us down."

Drawing his pistol, Drew checked his ammunition and started moving toward the spot where the shot had come from. Naturally Dayton wouldn't still be in the same place waiting for Drew to come after him. Not too far ahead, though, Drew found the ejected shells.

Standing quietly, Drew listened for other steps in the rocks. But all that he heard was the wind. The only movement he saw was buzzards circling not too far away over some dead animal.

Drew knew that Dayton had to be close. He couldn't have gone too far in such a short time. Drew hadn't spent that much time with Tag. Still, he stood quietly and listened. Nothing.

Drew felt as though he was in a no man's land, standing there competely alone with no human sounds other than his own breathing and the thundering of his heart in his ears. The afternoon sun glared down on him and his shirt stuck to his body.

What's Dayton waiting for? Drew asked himself angrily as he continued to listen. If he could see us enough to shoot and hit Tag, then he knows I'm alone. He walked a little further on and stopped to listen again.

Suddenly he was startled by a pebble falling down from the rocks above him. Jerking around, he saw Slade Dayton standing on an outcrop of rocks about fifteen feet up and ten feet away. His rifle was aimed directly at Drew's chest and there was no way he could miss from this distance. They were so close, in fact, that Drew could see the sweat trickling down Dayton's bearded face.

"Well, well, well," Dayton drawled with a sneering smile. "Looks like I finally got the drop on the great army scout. How does it feel to be on the other end of a gun, Williams? Too bad you don't have that purty little lady here to help you." With his thumb he cocked the hammer back on the rifle, taking careful aim at Drew.

Drew had come close to death many times, especially during the war. And each time was as scary as the first. Drew could almost see Dayton's finger squeezing down on the trigger.

They looked at each other for a long minute before Dayton said, "I told you I'd make you pay for my brother's death." Dayton lowered the rifle a little. "I killed that stinkin' Injun and the kid's got a busted leg. I don't know why he's helpin' you. But he's too young to die. That's why I didn't kill him. I could have, you know. Maybe he can find his way back to the fort. I'll put him on a horse after I kill you. You're all I'm after anyway."

Dayton raised the rifle up closer to his shoulder and with one eye squinted, looked down the long barrel at Drew. Then a thought struck him and he lowered the gun.

"I could shoot you in the leg," he said, squinting his eyes, "take your horse and leave you out here to starve to death. But I think I'll just gut shoot you and leave you for the buzzards. That way you can die and think at the same time. I've heard that gut shot is a terrible way to die."

Dayton laughed mirthfully as the horrible incident took place in his mind. A smirk crossed his bearded face as he thought about the malicious event. His eyes had the gleam of a mad man.

"Half Moon's not dead, Dayton," Drew implored in a tense voice. "If you'll give yourself up, you won't be in half as much trouble as you'll be if you kill me and if Tag dies."

"You're lyin', Williams," Dayton yelled, his voice echoing through the rocks. "You're just sayin' that to try to save your own hide. I know I killed that redskin. I saw him go down with my own eyes. I saw him bleed."

"You might have seen him go down," Drew insisted as calmly as the situation would allow. "There's no doubt you saw him bleeding. But you didn't kill him. You only shot him in the arm. He'll still be able to sign the agreement with Senator Dunbar."

The idea of reaching for his gun crossed Drew's mind for a brief second. But Dayton already had his rifle aimed at him with the hammer cocked. All he'd have to do was pull the trigger and that would be all for Drew.

But Drew knew that if he didn't do something quickly, Dayton was going to kill him and it would take a good while for him and Tag to be found. Colonel Walters knew where they were. But he wouldn't be in any big hurry to come looking for them. Drew didn't think that Dayton would be merciful enough to put Tag on a horse to go back to the fort.

Dayton would have his revenge on Drew and with Tom in the stockade, Slade would probably go on to Mexico and live like a rich man. No doubt, as Drew had told Tag, that the Daytons had a good bit of money from the hides, and Slade could live a pretty good life below the border.

"Look, Dayton, why don't you come down and go back to Fort Rather with us?" Drew asked, trying to reason with Dayton once more. "You haven't killed anybody yet. All you'll get is time in jail for attempted kidnapping."

"No, that ain't all I'll get and you know it," Dayton argued, spacing his words and shaking his head, a snarl on his lips. "You're forgettin' that I tried to kill or killed that Injun and that kid. They'd hang me for sure. You must think I'm real stupid."

Dayton threw back his head and laughed loudly, laughed for the last time. The movement threw him off balance and he stumbled, throwing his arms out, grasping at the air, trying to regain his balance. The rifle went off without hitting anything except the empty space above.

Drew, with a practiced hand and never being one to question fate, snatched his gun from the holster and from the hip, level, shot Slade Dayton square in the chest as he fell forward, the laugh frozen on his face.

Dayton hit the ground with a thud, landing in the dust and rocks at Drew's feet, his arms still flung out, the rifle a few feet away. Blood was already spreading across the front of Dayton's dirty shirt and trickling from his open mouth. His green eyes stared upward at nothing.

Bending down, Drew felt for the pulse under Dayton's throat. There was none. Slade Dayton was dead.

Wonder what Tom Dayton will think when he hears about this? Drew asked himself, still bent over the lifeless body of the outlaw who only a few minutes ago had held Drew's life in his hands.

Hearing a noise behind him, Drew stood up and turned around to see Tag hobbling up, using the rifle to lean on.

"I heard some shots and thought I'd come see what had happened," Tag said, resting against a large rock. "Are you all right?"

The color had returned to the boy's face. But he looked drawn. Drew knew that he was in pain by the way he gritted his teeth and his rapid breathing.

"Yeah, I'm all right," Drew replied, "but what if that had been me on the ground instead of Dayton?" Drew asked angrily, pointing toward the still form sprawled in the dirt.

"Do you realize what could have happened?"

"I guess he would have killed me," Tag answered simply, gaping at the dead man. His face turned white again and he began breathing harder. He swallowed a couple of times and turned away, bent over, and vomited.

Drew went to Tag, put his arm around his thin shoulders, took his own bandanna from his pocket and wiped Tag's face, then threw the soiled cloth away. "Are you all right, Tag?" Drew asked, sorry that he'd been so sharp with the boy.

"Yes," Tag replied weakly, avoiding Drew's eyes. "Are we goin' to take him back to Fort Rather or bury him here?"

"Well, there's no point in taking him all the way to the fort," Drew said dryly. "We can bury him here just as well."

Drew remembered seeing the shovel at the shack and ran back for it. When he returned, he was leading three horses, having found Dayton's in the rocks on the opposite way down. He also had Tag's cartridge belt. The blanket from the shack was thrown across Dayton's saddle.

When Drew reached Tag, the boy was still standing with his back to the body on the ground.

"Are you all right, Tag?" Drew asked again, taking him by the arm. The color rushed back into the boy's face. It was embarrassing that Drew thought he was a coward.

"Yes," he answered quickly but almost in a whisper. "I'm okay. It's just my leg."

Drew knew Tag was lying. He remembered

the first time he'd seen a dead man and he'd had the same sick feeling he knew Tag must have right now. But he didn't press the matter any further.

"Why don't you sit down there," Drew asked, pointing to the big boulder that Tag had been leaning against. "It won't take long to bury him."

Tag looked at him for a moment, a frown puckering his forehead. Then without comment, he shook his head.

"No," he said quickly. "I'll help you."

Drew dug a very shallow grave. The ground was too hard to dig one very deep. When Drew finally put the shovel down, Tag, using the rifle as a crutch, helped him draw Dayton's limp body over to the edge of the hole. Drew took the rank smelling blanket from Dayton's horse and wrapped it around the body. Drew picked up the dead man's shoulders and Tag picked up the feet by the cuffs and they dropped the outlaw's body into the grave and covered it with dirt and rocks.

Drew mounted and waited for Tag, who was still standing, looking down at the grave. If someone hadn't known what was there, they'd have thought it was just a pile of rocks, not realizing that a human being was beneath all of those rocks. Tag's face was almost expressionless except for a look of pain in his eyes. Drew thought it was from his leg.

"Tag," Drew asked anxiously, "are you sure you're all right?"

Tag nodded, took a deep breath, and got on the horse, his face twisting in pain when he raised his right leg over the saddle.

"You know," he said, without urging his horse to move, "that's a rotten way to end up." There was pity in the soft spoken voice.

"What do you mean?" Drew asked, feeling sorry for the boy. He'd probably just had his first bullet wound today and helped bury his first dead man.

"Well," Tag answered sadly, looking at Drew and then back at the grave, "to have lived such a life as he did and to end up in a makeshift grave out in the middle of nowhere without a preacher to say any words over you, where you'll stay forever, and nobody will every come to see your grave or care about it. We didn't even put a cross or a name on it."

Drew saw Tag swallow hard and blink his eyes quickly. For a moment Drew thought Tag was going to cry. A lump that felt as big as an egg came up in his own throat.

"Tag, the life that Dayton led is what caused him to end up like that," Drew said gently and nodding toward the grave. "He and his brothers knew right from wrong. You have to pay the price when you break the law. It's all right to feel compassion for people. But always try to keep things in the right perspective."

Tag nodded, and so that he wouldn't embarrass him any further, Drew reached out, caught up the reins of Dayton's horse, and kneed his horse into action.

If the situation had been different, it would have been a nice ride back to the fort in the beautiful sunset. The sun was a fiery red ball slipping down behind the purple mountains. There were still a few white clouds in the blue sky, and since the sun was going down, a breeze was beginning to drift across the land.

"We'd better get you back to the fort and to the doctor, Tag," Drew said to the silent youth riding behind him. "That leg must be giving you a fit."

When Tag didn't answer him, Drew turned around in the saddle. Tag looked up, nodded his answer, and dropped his head again.

Other than the creaking saddles and the horses' hooves on the ground, Drew led the way back to the fort in silence.

Chapter Eight

For the second time in two days, Drew was really glad to see the fort come into view. It was well after dark when they returned and the lights in various windows were a welcome sight. Without turning the horses into the corral, they went directly to the doctor's office. Tag had been silent the entire ride back. But when he saw the light in the doctor's office, he said, "I'm glad he's up."

Drew helped Tag dismount and in the light from the window, saw how pale the boy was. With his arm around Tag's shoulders, Drew steadied him as he moaned and gasped when he slid his right leg over the saddle.

Hearing them step up on the porch, Dr. Bryan opened the door. "What happened?" he asked in a monotone, seeing Tag's haggard and white face.

"He took a bullet in the leg, Doc," Drew explained, picking Tag up bodily and putting him on the examining table. The doctor cut off the bloody bandanna and pants leg, cleaned the wound, and put a bandage on it.

"How bad is it, Doc?" Tag asked in a trembling voice.

Dr. Bryan started to tell Tag that he was at the edge of death and have fun with the boy. He'd heard how Tag had conned his way into going with Drew and thought it would serve him right. But the wretched look on the boy's face changed his mind.

"Son, if this is the worst you'll ever get while you're out here in this God-forsaken place," the doctor said to Tag as he tied the gauze around his leg, "you'll be awfully lucky. But I can't see why Drew let you go with him and I can't see why you wanted to go on such a fool trip in the first place."

The old gray-haired doctor frowned as he cut off the ends of the gauze. He'd probably removed more bullets from men than Tag had years.

If it had been one of the young soldiers he was doctoring, he wouldn't have minded so much. But a boy like Tag who wanted to go just to prove that he was old enough riled the old man.

"Doc, I'll bet you weren't much older than Tag when you had to prove how brave you were," Drew said, standing by the table.

"Thanks, Drew," Tag said gratefully, looking up at him and blinking his eyes slowly and weakly.

The doctor, seeing the pallor on Tag's thin face, knew that the boy was still upset and nervous over his first real brush with death.

"Tag," he said kindly, patting the boy on shoulder, "only in rare cases will I do this.

I'm going to let you stay here in the office tonight." He was sure that Tag would feel much better just knowing a doctor was near.

"Thanks a lot, Doc," Tag replied, a weak smile on his face.

Drew helped Tag down from the table and into the extra bedroom. When Tag was in bed and made comfortable, Drew went to Walters' office.

He had to knock several times before any sounds could be heard from inside. Finally, Walters opened the door, dressed in pants with his red nightshirt stuffed down in them and house slippers. Rubbing sleep from his eyes with one hand, Walters motioned Drew to a chair with the other.

"Did you get Dayton?" Walters asked, trying to suppress a yawn.

"Yes," Drew replied wearily, beginning to feel the effect of so many hours in the saddle; the happenings of today were getting to him. "I had to kill him," Drew continued when Walters didn't explain how he meant 'get Dayton.' "I tried to reason with him. But he wouldn't listen. If he hadn't slipped on a rock, he would have gut shot me and left me out there to die. He shot Tag in the leg and said that he'd put Tag on his horse and let him come back here—but I doubt he would really have done it. And besides, Tag couldn't have gotten back here alone."

"How is the boy?" Walters asked without much real concern, while he rubbed his sleepy eyes again.

"Oh, he was more scared than hurt," Drew

told him with a slight smile. "Helping bury his first dead man didn't help much either. But he'll be okay." Drew stood up, stretched, and walked to the door. "How's Half Moon?"

"He's fine," Walters said in a drowsy voice. "A little mad at being taken by one man when one woman had guarded two men with no trouble. But there's a problem."

Drew was already at the door with his hand on the know when Walters' statement stopped him in his tracks.

"What problem?" Drew demanded, turning around slowly, giving Walters a level look.

"Half Moon says he won't sign the agreement," Walters answered, dropping his gaze to the floor. Then he raised his eyes to give Drew a sheepish look.

Anger swept over Drew as he stood looking at Walters sitting so calmly in the chair. He didn't seem very concerned about the matter after so much trouble had been taken to get the Indians to Fort Rather to meet Senator Dunbar. After all, that was the object.

"Why won't he sign?" Drew asked slowly, an edge in his voice. Turning around slowly, Drew came back to the colonel.

"Well," Walters answered, "because he feels that the agreement won't hold up now. He's mad because he'd given you his word that he'd get the Daytons here safely and one of them tried to kill him."

"Half Moon knew the risks involved when he volunteered to bring the Daytons here," Drew said flatly. "He'd have done the same thing if the tables were turned. What are you going to do about it?"

"Me!" Walters asked, fully awake now and raising his eyebrows. "I though maybe you'd talk to him."

"Not me," Drew refused coldly. "I've done my job. The rest is entirely up to you and Senator Dunbar. By the way," he said, going back to the door and opening it, "is she ... I mean ... are they here yet?"

"Yes, she's ... I mean ... they're here," Walters answered mockingly. "Now get out of here and let me get some sleep."

Drew slammed the door shut behind him and stepped out on the porch. The cool night air on his face helped calm down his temper. But he was still disgusted with Walters. That man has about as much business being in charge of anything as I do with a herd of goats, Drew muttered to himself.

Crossing the yard to the barracks, Drew saw an unfamiliar stage in front of the guest quarters. Being a curious man, he ambled over to it.

Even in the dark, it was easy to tell that the stage had been made to order. The senator's crest was emblazoned on the door that he opened on well-oiled hinges. He looked inside and the fragrance of lilacs brought immediate thoughts of Melissa.

He struck a match and looked further inside, whistling at what he saw. Thickly padded, dark brown leather seats wide enough to accommodate four, with removable arm rests, were on each side of the spacious vehicle. Instead of the usual bare wooden floor, there was a light brown carpet. The overhead was done in yellow and brown tapestry.

Leather roll flaps over each of the six windows were the only condescending things about the stage. Even the ties that held the flaps up were out of brown rolled cord. There were even foot rests that pulled out from under the seats.

When this senator travels, Drew thought, closing the door, he really does it in style. No wonder Melissa was so put out at having to ride a horse. I'd have thrown a fit, too, if I had to give up conveniences like this.

He glanced toward the guest quarters and was disappointed to see that the windows were dark. He'd hoped to see Melissa for a few minutes at least before going to bed. But there was always tomorrow and surely Walters wouldn't send him out before the agreement signing.

The windows in the barracks were ablaze and a little voice in the back of Drew's mind told him who'd be there.

Sure enough, Charles Sinclair was sitting at the long table, a full cup of coffee before him.

"I want to talk to you, Williams," Sinclair said to Drew as soon as he walked through the door, the old assertiveness back in his voice.

"What is it?" Drew asked tonelessly. He took off his hat and began unbuttoning his shirt.

"Well, if I'd known that you really needed

some help in bringing that desperado back, I'd have gone with you."

"Sinclair," Drew replied wearily, "you'd have fainted if I'd asked you to go with me—which I wouldn't have done in the first place." Drew stood looking down at the Englishman sitting at the table, his legs crossed. His clothes, as usual, were immaculate.

"I beg your pardon," Sinclair gasped, springing to his feet. A fire blazed in his brown eyes and his fair face became flushed. He'd had the riding crop on the bench beside him and in one motion jerked it up and lashed out at Drew. The crop whistled as it swished through the air.

Drew hadn't anticipated the move and didn't have time to duck. The small end of the crop caught him across the left side of his face.

For a moment, Drew and Sinclair stared at each other, surprise in the brown eyes of Sinclair, a burning rage in Drew's blue eyes.

Slowly raising his left hand, Drew touched his face, then lowered his hand. The sight of his own blood on his own hand broke the spell.

Reaching out with his right hand, Drew snatched the crop from Sinclair, broke it in half over his knee, and slung the pieces across the room. Then he grabbed Sinclair by the front of his cream-colored shirt and jerked him forward.

"Sinclair, if you weren't such a coward, I'd beat you to a pulp," Drew growled, breathing hard in rage. "But you're not going to get away with that."

Drew switched hands on the shirt and then with the fury of a storm, slapped Sinclair first on the left side of his face with the open hand and then let him have it again with the back of the hand on the right side of his face.

The print of Drew's hand stood out on Sinclair's face like a red sign. Drew let go of the man and he dropped to the floor on his knees. Sinclair shook his head and looked up at Drew, a mixture of fear and shock all over his face. A trickle of blood oozed from his mouth and Drew's hand prints became more prominent on his fair face.

"I wish that you'd hit me with your fists instead, Williams," Sinclair whined, holding his bruised face in both hands. "For one man to slap another is considered a terrible insult in civilized circles. Gentlemen use their fists."

"Well, I've never been considered very civilized," Drew said coldly, looking down at Sinclair, his eyes blazing with blue fire. "But I'll tell you one thing," Drew threatened, pointing his finger at Sinclair, "you ever raise a crop to me again, I'll kill you. Now the best place for you is in the guest quarters."

Only a few men had been in the barracks and they had all watched silently as the happenings took place. Sinclair had bragged to them about his brave riding club in England and they were glad to see him get his.

Sinclair walked across the floor without looking at anyone, picked up the pieces of his treasured riding crop, and rushed out the door, slamming it behind him.

Before the men could say anything to Drew,

he picked up his hat and strode down to the end of the barracks to his bunk. Taking off his shirt, boots, and socks, and stretching out on the bunk, he went to sleep.

Drew was up early the next morning after a good night's sleep. Awakening as usual before the sun was up, he bathed and shaved, getting mad all over again when he looked at the red welt on his face. I hope I don't see Sinclair today, Drew thought angrily as he gently patted his sore face dry. Then he dressed in fresh clothes. Thinking about wearing the blue suit, he gave it up as being a little too much. Besides, it would be too hot. So instead he wore tan pants, a light blue shirt, the well-worn moccasin boots, and the same old battered hat with the new hole in it.

He'd hoped to see Melissa at breakfast. His heart skipped a couple of beats just thinking about seeing her. But as he was on his way to the mess hall, he saw a private carrying a tray toward the guest quarters and knew that seeing her was out of the question.

Senator Dunbar came in while Drew was finishing his coffee and sat down beside him at the long table.

"I didn't expect you to be here until tomorrow," Drew said, taking a sip of coffee and putting the cup down.

"I didn't either," Dunbar replied with a half smile. "But the morning after my birthday party, Melissa was up at a most unusual early hour and insisted that we leave just after breakfast."

"What reason did she give for wanting to

come back here so soon?" Drew asked, holding his breath, glancing sideways at the senator, a half smile, half frown on his face.

"Well, she said that as long as the Indians were already here, we shouldn't take the chance that Half Moon might change his mind about signing the agreement."

With the mention of Half Moon and the agreement, Drew remembered what Colonel Walters had told him last night.

"Have you seen the colonel or Half Moon this morning?" Drew asked hesitantly.

"Yes," Dunbar replied, bewildered at the look on Drew's face. "I saw the colonel and Half Moon going toward Walters' office a few minutes ago. Walters plans to have the ceremonies today at one instead of waiting until tomorrow as planned."

Wonder what Walters told Half Moon to get him to sign the agreement? Drew asked himself as he left the mess hall. I'm not going to worry about it. That's Walters' and Dunbar's problem. I've done my job.

Apparently they were really going to have the signing because people began coming from buildings at one and milling around like they were waiting for something to happen.

Drew saw Melissa's father escort her across the yard to stand with the other ladies. When she saw Drew, she smiled warmly at him and waved. There wasn't time for any conversation. Looking around the crowd, Drew noticed that Charles Sinclair was nowhere in sight.

Drew didn't know and couldn't guess what

the colonel had told Half Moon. But the three men who came to the colonel's office together were greeted by applause.

The festivities were to begin at one and it was precisely on the hour when the three men emerged from Walters' office.

Colonel Walters was decked out in his best blue uniform. His black boots were polished to a bright luster and the gold buttons on his coat sparkled in the sun.

Senator Dunbar had changed from his brown suit to a gray broadcloth trimmed in black. His thick gray hair was neatly combed and looked like silver in the bright sunlight.

Chief Half Moon, his left arm in a sling, was as well dressed in his buckskin, beads, and feathers as were the other men. His clothes were white and he wore the same headdress he had on when Drew saw him the other day. His black hair hung in thick coils on each side of his bronze face. Drew thought he looked a little pale but his black eyes were bright and had an undefinable gleam in them.

A desk had been placed on the ground in front of the colonel's office. Three chairs were behind it, and the stars and stripes and a company flag hung limply on each side of the desk. Two lances, with feathers on the end, were stuck in the ground on each side of the flags.

"Mr. Williams," Senator Dunbar said to Drew, shaking his hand with ceremony, "since you've had such an important part in this, I think that you should be here at the desk with us."

"Thank you, sir," Drew said, feeling surprised and embarrassed. He didn't like being in the center of things, but he took the place indicated behind Colonel Walters.

"After I talked to Half Moon this morning," Colonel Walters said, turning around to face Drew, "he decided to sign the agreement. But he just wanted to sign it and then leave. He said he was in a hurry to get back to his village. I guess he wants the medicine man to have a look at his arm," Walters smirked.

Curiosity began eating at Drew. He was dying to know what Walters had told Half Moon to get him to sign the agreement. There was a look about Walters that Drew didn't understand. Like he knew a secret but there was no way he'd tell. But Drew wouldn't give the colonel the satisfaction of asking, especially not right now. And he certainly wouldn't ask Half Moon.

Drew really didn't blame Half Moon for not wanting to sign an agreement with the white man. There had been enough agreements and treaties signed in years past between the Indians and the government for one thing or another to paper the walls of Colonel Walters' office. Not many of them had ever held up and the Indians were always on the losing end of the stick.

"But I insisted on a ceremony," Walters continued pettishly. "I thought it'd look more important in front of the senator if we had a bugler and a drummer and a drill by an honor guard." He looked so pleased with himself that Drew wanted to shake him. But he just shook his head instead.

The three men sat down at the table with Senator Dunbar in the middle. Drew stood directly behind Walters and Little Bear behind Half Moon.

When everyone was in their places, Colonel Walters nodded to the bugler. The young man took the highly polished brass horn from under his arm and blew a few notes on it that really didn't amount to much. The drummer followed with a brisk drum roll. When each man finished his part, he saluted and stepped back in line.

"It's on occasions like this," the colonel began, standing up and sounding rehearsed, "that we're all glad to be together. We're here today to try and bring about a better understanding between the white man and the Indian."

Drew glanced over at Half Moon and his bronze face was as immobile as usual. I wonder how many times he's heard that before? Drew asked himself.

Senator Dunbar was beginning to sweat in the glaring sun. The sky was clear and there wasn't a breath of air anywhere. How could anybody in their right mind be glad to be out in such heat? Dunbar took a white handkerchief from his pocket, mopped his face, and cast a skeptical look up at Walters.

Drew knew how much Walters liked being the center of attention and would talk as long as possible. Walters seemed to be absolutely unaware of the heat even though sweat was pouring down his flushed face.

Drew, like Half Moon and possibly Senator Dunbar, saw no reason for such a long and drawn-out affair. The agreement could have been signed just as effectively in Walters' office and Drew could have been with Melissa.

Thinking of her, Drew looked over to the barracks where the women were standing. Since Indians believed that women had no business in men's affairs, none had been invited to attend the ceremony directly, including Melissa, although they were permitted to watch from a distance.

There were about fifteen or so ladies. But it was easy to pick her out of the group. If she hadn't been standing in front, he still wouldn't have had any trouble finding her. She seemed to stand out like a flower among thorns. Not that any of the other ladies were ugly. But when one woman, with hair the color of honey and wearing a blue dress that came just below the throat, and you knew that she was looking directly at you with a gleam in her eyes, a man really didn't pay too much attention to anyone else.

A voice droning on and on brought Drew's thoughts back to the men at the desk in front of him. Colonel Walters was still going strong about better times and relations between the races.

Enough was enough, Drew decided. Clearing his throat, he eased his right hand out touching the colonel on the back. Drew was standing close enough behind Walters so that the movement wasn't noticed by anyone except Dunbar, who turned slightly, giving Drew a nod and a grateful smile.

"Now," Walters said quickly and clearing

his throat, taking the hint, "I'd like to introduce Rance Dunbar, the senator of the great Arizona Territory . . . "

"Thank you, Colonel Walters," Dunbar said, standing up before the colonel was really finished. "It's very hot out here and I know we all would like to be inside. Especially Chief Half Moon, who had the misfortune of being shot by one of the men who made this agreement necessary."

At hearing his name called unexpectedly, Half Moon jerked his head up to look at Senator Dunbar. He was certainly surprised by this statement. For a moment his black eyes widened and a pink cast rose beneath his bronze skin. He probably wasn't used to having such courtesies bestowed upon him by a white man and such a powerful man as a senator.

"My daughter and I are very happy to be here at Fort Rather for this auspicious occasion," Dunbar went on, extending his arm in the direction of Melissa. "I know there have been other treaties signed at other ceremonies such as this. I only hope that this one will last longer than most of them have."

Dunbar wiped his face again and turned toward Half Moon.

"Sir," Dunbar said with a genuine smile, "would you care to say something?"

For a moment the chief hesitated. Then rising slowly to his feet, he let his gaze sweep the entire fort and the mountains beyond.

"My people depend on buffalo for life," he said in a slow voice. "If we were at my village, everywhere you look are sign of buffalo. Our homes, clothes, moccasins, and food come from buffalo. But here are no signs. White man not need buffalo like Indian. White man only want buffalo for hide. Meat is left out in the sun and spoils. But not all white man bad, though," he went on, turning around and looking at Drew with a pleasant expression. "Not all Indians bad. Maybe this treaty will be good thing."

As the chief sat down, from out of nowhere a cloud passed over the sun and nobody could keep from looking up and watch it scutter across the blue sky.

I hope that cloud isn't a bad omen, Drew thought, still bewildered at Half Moon's look. He had no idea what the Indian meant by it.

Senator Dunbar, wanting to hurry things along and get out of the hot sun, pulled the paper in front of him and signed his name with a flurry. Then Colonel Walters signed. Drew had thought all of the time that Half Moon would make a mark and someone else would write his name under the mark. But he was amazed to see the chief pick up the feathered pen and write his name smoothly and clearly without any help. I wonder where he learned to write? Drew mused, knowing that he wouldn't rest until his curiosity was satisfied.

Dunbar took the agreement, folded it, and put it in a brown envelope and then in his inside coat pocket. Then he started to push his chair back and leave the table. Half Moon had also stood up.

"Wait," the colonel wailed, "we haven't had our honor guard drill yet."

If looks could kill, the one Walters got from Dunbar would have really finished him off.

"If he wasn't a colonel," Dunbar said under his breath to Drew, "and if we hadn't just signed a sort of peace treaty, I swear I'd shoot him."

Drew and Half Moon nodded at the same time and grinned at the senator.

Reluctantly, Dunbar and Half Moon sat down. The senator nodded his wet face again as six smartly dressed corporals snapped to attention and under the direction from a seventh, went through a procedure of presenting arms, twirling guns, and other intricate movements.

Once the six men turned around facing the men at the table. Half Moon jerked back and turned pale as the six guns were aimed directly at him. But he regained his composure as the young men continued with the exercise. With it being so hot, nobody was really impressed except Colonel Walters.

When the drill was finally finished and the desk and chairs were carried inside, all of the men shook hands. Colonel Walters and Senator Dunbar went inside. Half Moon and Little Bear mounted their horses that the other Indians had been holding. Still very curious about Half Moon's ability to write, Drew had to find out how and when he'd learned.

"Chief," Drew asked, approaching the Indians who were already mounted, "I'd like to ask you a question if I may?"

"Of course," Half Moon said, looking down at him, a different, a slightly different, expression crossing his face and making his eyes less stonelike.

"I noticed a while ago that you could write," Drew said, "and I was wondering how you learned. Not many Indians write English, you know?" Drew didn't want Half Moon to get the impression that he thought all Indians were ignorant by not being able to read or write anything.

"Some years past," Half Moon answered, gazing off into the distance, "a white man rode through village. He was lost, almost starved, and very sick. My father was chief. He had white man doctored. In payment, white man taught me to read and write."

When Half Moon had finished talking, he faced Drew again and looked over his shoulder. This time a real smile brightened his face revealing white teeth.

"Why do you waste time with Indian?" he asked, looking directly at Drew. Drew turned around to see what he was talking about. Melissa was still standing on the porch in front of the barracks where she'd been during the signing of the agreement. Only this time she was alone. Drew knew she was waiting for him and a warm tingle ran over him.

"Better not keep her waiting," Half Moon said, a twinkle in his black eyes. "That woman can guard two men with one gun."

"I know," Drew said, grinning back at him. Drew extended his hand and Half Moon shook it in a firm grip. Raising his hand in a final gesture, Half Moon kneed his horse into motion and the rest of the Indians fell into single file behind him. Half Moon went a few paces, turned and came back to Drew who'd started toward Melissa.

"I hope first child is girl," Half Moon said complacently when he'd stopped by Drew. "Little Half Moon good name for a girl. White people not care which child come first." Half Moon looked questionably at Drew when his eyes almost fell out of his head and his mouth popped open without any words coming out.

"What are you talking about?" Drew asked slowly when he finally found his voice. He stood gaping up at the chief.

"Colonel Walters promise if I sign agreement, which I no going to do, that daughter of Senator Dunbar and army scout would name first child after me. So I sign. Never had a white child named for me before."

With that simple explanation, simple to the Indian anyway, Half Moon turned and loped out of the yard, his men behind him.

Drew stood there for a few minutes, still in a state of absolute shock. How in the world was he going to be able to face Melissa after hearing a thing like that? Maybe she didn't know about it. He knew that she was waiting for him and he walked slowly toward her. Taking off his hat, he stepped up on the porch beside her.

"How did you like the ... uh ... ceremony?" he asked uncertainly, smiling down at her.

"Is that what it was?" she asked in a soft voice, returning his smile, enjoying the effect she knew she was having on him. "I've seen more impressive ceremonies with children.

What happened to your face?" she asked, reaching up and touching the welt gently.

"Charles Sinclair did that yesterday with what used to be a riding crop," Drew told her, enjoying her concern.

"Did you beat him up?" she asked expectantly.

"Not really," Drew replied. "I slapped him a couple of times and broke the crop. He told me how uncivilized I was."

From the way she talked, Drew surmised that she didn't know about the promise Colonel Walters had made Chief Half Moon.

"It seems that Colonel Walters threw the ceremony together for his own satisfaction," she said. "My father told me that he and Half Moon had just wanted to sign the agreement in the colonel's office. But Walters would have none of it. But I guess the main thing is that an agreement has been signed. I just hope that it works for a while at least."

"If the government was as concerned about treaties lasting between them and the Indians," Drew said, finding his voice and wondering if she was pretending not to know what Walters had told Half Moon, "as civilians are, maybe things would be different."

"What happened to the other Dayton men?" she asked, seeming content to stand there in the heat talking to him.

Drew told her about Slade getting a gun, shooting Half Moon, and escaping day before yesterday.

"Is that what happened to Half Moon?" she asked, her eyes going big and wide in real surprise. "When did you find out about this?" she asked.

"Just after I got back to the fort yesterday," Drew answered, pleased that she was really interested in what he'd been doing. He'd always thought that a woman only wanted to talk about themselves and things that just concerned women, "and about two hours before Tag and I went after him."

"Tag?" she asked, reaching out and flicking some dust from his shoulders. "Isn't he the one you bought those clothes from for me?"

Drew only nodded his head. Her touch couldn't have burned any more than a hot poker. While the signing was taking place, Drew had been conscious of how hot it was. Now that he was alone with Melissa, the heat was the furthest thing from his mind. She didn't seem to be in any hurry to go inside either.

"Was Tag out here during the signing?" Melissa asked.

"No," Drew replied, "he's in bed at the doctor's office. He got shot in the leg yesterday when he went with me after Slade Dayton."

"Why did you let him do such a foolish thing as that?" she asked, a frown wrinkling her smooth features.

"Because he kept insisting," Drew replied. "He's at least eighteen and he has to grow up sometime."

"He must be quite a young man," she said smiling. "I'd like to go and see him. I want to thank him for selling his clothes to you for me."

They were standing not too far from the guardhouse with no other thoughts on their minds than just being together. Then the shot rang out.

The bullet caught Drew in the left shoulder, knocking him to his knees, and he fell against Melissa's legs. His hat dropped from his limp fingers, bounced on the porch, and rolled off into the dust.

"Drew!" Melissa screamed, dropping down by him on the porch and throwing her arms around him, pulling him tightly against her. "Drew," she screamed again.

Melissa's screams and the shot brought armed soldiers racing out of the barracks and they stopped beside Drew and Melissa.

"The shot came from there," she said, nodding toward the guardhouse, still holding Drew in her arms. Drew didn't think he was hurt all that much, but why pass up this opportunity?

The soldiers rushed toward the guardhouse and three shots rang out in rapid succession. Then the guardhouse door opened and two of the soldiers emerged, carrying the limp body of Tom Dayton.

Colonel Walters and Senator Dunbar came tearing out of the colonel's office and Dunbar rushed over to Drew and helped him to his feet. Melissa stepped off the porch, picked up his hat, and put her arm around his waist.

A red spot stained his shirt and blood had begun running down his arm and dripping on the porch.

"What happened?" Walters asked, looking around frantically.

"Somebody shot me," Drew replied slowly, a bewildered daze in his eyes. He shook his head unbelieving.

"Who? From where?" Walters asked, glancing nervously around the fort and ducking behind a post.

"Tom Dayton shot him," the private named Pete answered. He approached them looking rumpled, as though he'd been in a fight.

"How did he get a gun?" Drew asked reflectively. Dayton hadn't been under any special guard. But they knew that he didn't have a gun.

"I should have known better," Pete said, rubbing his head where a knot was beginning to raise.

"Should have known better?" Dunbar repeated, skeptically. "What do you mean? What did you do, young man?"

"Oh, I was passin' the guardhouse just after the Indians left," Pete recounted, "and I heard someone moanin'. I knew it was comin' from Dayton's cell. But I thought maybe he was sick. I went in and . . ."

"And he grabbed you, took your gun, and shot me with it," Drew interrupted through clenched teeth. He didn't know which feeling was greater: the pain in his shoulder or his anger at the young private's foolish action. He decided that if the pain in his shoulder wasn't so much, he'd take great pleasure in letting Pete have it right across the jaw.

"Is Dayton dead?" Walters asked, raising

his voice to the privates standing by the still body on the ground. One of the soldiers nodded without saying anything.

"Weren't there three Daytons?" Melissa asked, holding to Drew's arm.

"Yes," Colonel Walters answered, a slight smile on his face. "Now we won't have as much trouble enforcing that treaty with the Indians."

"Walters," Senator Dunbar said, icy disgust in his voice, "with all of the Daytons dead, we won't really need the agreement." The senator mopped his face, spun around, and went back into the colonel's office.

"You'd better get over to the doctor and let him take a look at your shoulder," Melissa said softly, a tender expression in her brown eyes.

"Will you go with me?" Drew asked, an engaging look in his blue eyes.

"Why?" she asked, looking up at him and not caring that Colonel Walters was still listening.

"Well," he said, looking down at her with a heart-stopping gaze, "with a bullet in my left arm and you holding to the other one, there might be a snake you'll have to throw a rock at."

Melissa dropped her arm in mock indignation. "How long are you going to remind me about that snake?" she asked, smiling fondly and wrinkling her nose up at him.

"Forever, I hope, Melissa," he said, calling her by her given name for the first time and holding out his right arm for her to take again.

"Forever is a long time, Drew," she said, pressing his arm against her side as they walked toward the doctor's office.

"Did Half Moon tell you about the agreement, Williams?" Walters called out to them as they walked across the yard. "If he did, you'd better tell her. If he didn't, I'll tell you both."

"He told me," Drew said loudly, without looking back.

"What agreement?" Melissa asked puzzled, looking up at him.

"Well," he drawled, almost forgetting the pain in his arm as the idea took shape in his mind, "it looks as though you and I will have to get married."

"Get married!" she cried in astonishment, her eyes big and round. She tugged at his arm and they stopped walking. "Why?" She blushed at the question. "I know why. But what does the colonel have to say about it?"

"Well, you know that Half Moon wasn't going to sign the agreement?" Drew said. Melissa shook her head.

"Colonel Walters wanted me to talk to him and get him to change his mind," Drew went on. "I told him that it was up to him and your father. I didn't know what Walters told the chief until after the signing. He promised Half Moon that if he'd sign the agreement, that our first child, yours and mine, would be named for him. So he signed."

Melissa stopped walking, dropped her arm, and for a moment looked up at Drew with a blankness in her eyes. Dropping her gaze to the ground for a minute, she slowly raised her head, beginning to grin. Then she nodded.

"Well, we certainly can't disappoint Chief Half Moon, and our grandchildren must hear all about it like you said before. By the way," she scolded, "you have some explaining to do anyway."

"About what?" Drew asked, frowning down at her, wondering what she meant.

"I want to know why I didn't have a blue dress to wear at Papa's party. If he hadn't surprised me with a new one, I'd have been there in Tag's old clothes."

"I'll tell you all about it someday," Drew answered, throwing back his head and laughing. They opened the door and walked into the doctor's office.

THE END

SPECTACULAR SERIES

NAZI INTERROGATOR (649, $2.95)
by Raymond F. Toliver
The terror, the fear, the brutal treatment, and mental torture of WWII prisoners are all revealed in this first-hand account of the Luftwaffe's master interrogator.

THE SGT. #3: BLOODY BUSH (647, $2.25)
by Gordon Davis
In this third exciting episode, Sgt. C.J. Mahoney is put to his deadliest test when he's assigned to bail out the First Battalion in Normandy's savage Battle of the Hedgerows.

SHELTER #3: CHAIN GANG KILL (658, $1.95)
by Paul Ledd
Shelter finds himself "wanted" by a member of the death battalion who double-crossed him seven years before *and* by a fiery wench. Bound by lust, Shelter aims to please; burning with vengeance, he seeks to kill!

GUNN #3: DEATH'S HEAD TRAIL (648, $1.95)
by Jory Sherman
When Gunn stops off in Bannack City he finds plenty of gold, girls, and a gunslingin' outlaw who wants it all. With his hands on his holster and his eyes on the sumptuous Angela Larkin, Gunn goes off hot—on his enemy's trail!

Available wherever paperbacks are sold, or order direct from the Publisher. Send cover price plus 50¢ per copy for mailing and handling to Zebra Books, 21 East 40th Street, New York, N.Y. 10016. DO NOT SEND CASH!

THE INCREDIBLE STRATEGIES, STUNNING VICTORIES, AND AGONIZING DEFEATS OF THE SECOND WORLD WAR!

ON VALOR'S SIDE   (574, $2.75)
by T. Grady Gallant
From the initial rigors of Parris Island to the actual combat conditions of Guadalcanal—a true first-hand account of what it was like to be a Marine during World War II.

THE RACE FOR THE RHINE   (460, $2.50)
by Alexander McKee
As the Allies pushed on and the Nazis retreated, Hitler's orders came—blow the Rhine bridges or be shot!

THE SGT. #1: DEATH TRAIN   (600, $2.25)
by Gordon Davis
The first in a new World War II series featuring the action-crammed exploits of the Sergeant, C.J. Mahoney, the big, brawling career GI, the almost-perfect killing machine who, with a handful of *maquis*, steals an explosive laden train and heads for a fateful rendezvous in a tunnel of death.

THE BATTLE OF ARNHEM   (538, $2.50)
by Cornelis Bauer
A fully documented narrative that reveals the horror—and heroism—of the British fiasco that became one of World War II's bloodiest battles . . . THE BATTLE OF ARNHEM.

Available wherever paperbacks are sold, or order direct from the Publisher. Send cover price plus 50¢ per copy for mailing and handling to Zebra Books, 21 East 40th Street, New York, N.Y. 10016. DO NOT SEND CASH!

DISASTER NOVELS

EPIDEMIC! (644, $2.50)
by Larry R. Leichter, M.D.
From coast to coast, beach to beach, the killer virus spread. Diagnosed as a strain of meningitis, it did not respond to treatment—and no one could stop it from becoming the world's most terrifying epidemic!

FIRE MOUNTAIN (646, $2.50)
by Janet Cullen-Tanaka
Everyone refused to listen but hour by hour, yard by yard, the cracks and fissures in Mt. Rainer grew. Within hours the half-million-year-old volcano rose from its sleep, causing one of the most cataclysmic eruptions of all time.

GHOST SUB (655, $2.50)
by Roger E. Herst
The U.S.S. *Amundsen* is on the most dangerous patrol since World War II—it is equipped with deadly weapons . . . and nothing less than a nuclear holocaust hangs in the balance.

AVALANCHE (672, $2.50)
by Max Steele
Disaster strikes at the biggest and newest ski resort in the Rocky Mountains. It is New Year's eve and the glamorous and glittering ski people find themselves trapped between a wall of fire and a mountain of impenetrable snow.

Available wherever paperbacks are sold, or order direct from the Publisher. Send cover price plus 50¢ per copy for mailing and handling to Zebra Books, 21 East 40th Street, New York, N.Y. 10016. DO NOT SEND CASH!

READ THESE ZEBRA BEST SELLERS

THE BIG NEEDLE (512, $2.25)
by Ken Follett
Innocent people were being terrorized, homes were being destroyed—and all too often—because the most powerful organization in the world was thirsting for one man's blood. By the author of *The Eye of the Needle*.

NEW YORK ONE (556, $2.25)
by Lawrence Levine
Buried deep within the tunnels of Grand Central Station lies the most powerful money center of the world. Only a handful of people knows it exists—and one of them wants it destroyed!

ERUPTION (614, $2.75)
by Paul Patchick
For fifty years the volcano lay dorment, smoldering, bubbling, building. Now there was no stopping it from becoming the most destructive eruption ever to hit the western hemisphere—or anywhere else in the entire world!

DONAHUE! (570, $2.25)
by Jason Bonderoff
The intimate and revealing biography of Americas #1 daytime TV host—his life, his loves, and the issues and answers behind the Donahue legend.

Available wherever paperbacks are sold, or order direct from the Publisher. Send cover price plus 50¢ per copy for mailing and handling to Zebra Books, 21 East 40th Street, New York, N.Y. 10016. DO NOT SEND CASH!

READ THESE HORRIFYING BEST SELLERS!

THE NEST (662, $2.50)
by Gregory A. Douglas
An ordinary garbage dump in a small quiet town becomes the site of incredible horror when a change in poison control causes huge mutant creatures to leave their nest in search of human flesh.

CHERRON (700, $2.50)
by Sharon Combes
A young girl, taunted and teased for her physical imperfections, uses her telekinetic powers to wreak bloody vengeance on her tormentors—body and soul!

LONG NIGHT (515, $2.25)
by P. B. Gallagher
An innocent relationship turns into a horrifying nightmare of terror when a beautiful young woman falls victim to a man seeking revenge for his father's death.

CALY (624, $2.50)
by Sharon Combes
When Ian Donovan and Caly St. John arrive at the eerie Simpson House in Maine, they open a door and release a ghost woman who leads them beyond terror and toward the most gruesome, grisly experience that anyone could ever imagine.

THE SIN (479, $2.50)
by Robert Vaughan
A small town becomes the victim of a young woman's strange sensual powers leading to unnatural deaths.

Available wherever paperbacks are sold, or order direct from the Publilsher. Send cover price plus 50¢ per copy for mailing and handling to Zebra Books, 21 East 40th Street, New York, N.Y. 10016. DO NOT SEND CASH!